NOTTING HILL GATE

4 Basic

Klassenarbeitstrainer

Erarbeitet von

Eva Cloer (Bremen),
Katrin Kremer (Remscheid),
Katja Werthen-Giles (Thedinghausen)

Diesterweg
westermann

NOTTING HILL GATE 4 Basic

Für Klasse 8 an Gesamtschulen und anderen integrierenden Schulformen

Materialien für Schülerinnen und Schüler

- Textbook 978-3-425-14604-1
- Workbook mit Lernsoftware und Audio-CD 978-3-425-14624-9
- Workbook mit Audio-CD 978-3-425-14614-0
- Lernsoftware Einzelplatzlizenz 978-3-425-14654-6
- Vocab-App (Android-Version) WEB-425-14664
- Vocab-App (iOS-Version) WEB-425-13970
- Inklusions- und Fördermaterialien mit Audio-CD 978-3-425-14674-4
- Zoom-App www.zoom-app.de
- BiBox – Schüler-Einzellizenz WEB-425-30007

Fördert individuell – passt zum Schulbuch
Optimal für den Einsatz im Unterricht mit Notting Hill Gate! Stärken erkennen, Defizite beheben. Online-Lernstandsdiagnose und Auswertung auf Basis der aktuellen Bildungsstandards. Individuell zusammengestellte Fördermaterialien.

www.diesterweg.de/diagnose Online-Diagnose

Materialien für Lehrkräfte

- Lehrerfassung zum Schülerband 978-3-425-13996-8
- Teacher's Manual 978-3-425-14904-2
- Vorschläge für Lernerfolgskontrollen mit CD-ROM 978-3-425-14944-8
- Workbook mit Lösungen und Audio-CD 978-3-425-14914-1
- Audio-CD für Lehrkräfte 978-3-425-14934-9
- DVD für Lehrkräfte 978-3-425-14824-3
- Kopiervorlagen 978-3-425-14954-7
- Module für projektorientierten Unterricht Klasse 7/8 978-3-425-14073-5
- BiBox – Digitale Unterrichtsmaterialien Einzellizenz WEB-425-14994 Kollegiumslizenz WEB-425-14998 DVD-ROM-Version 978-3-425-14886-1
- Lernsoftware Schullizenz 978-3-425-14984-4

westermann GRUPPE

Druck A[1] / Jahr 2018
Alle Drucke der Serie A sind im Unterricht parallel verwendbar.

Redaktion: lüra – Klemt & Mues GbR, Wuppertal
Illustrationen: Ulf Marckwort, Kassel
Umschlaggestaltung: blum design und kommunikation GmbH, Hamburg
Umschlagfoto: Dirk Schmidt/dsphotos.de
Layoutkonzeption: tiff.any GmbH, Berlin
Druck und Bindung: westermann druck GmbH, Braunschweig

ISBN 978-3-425-**14964**-2

So arbeitest du mit dem Klassenarbeitstrainer zu *Notting Hill Gate 4 Basic*

Tipp Lies die Tipp-Kästen zu jeder Aufgabe genau durch. Sie geben dir **Schritt-für-Schritt-Hinweise** zum Lösen der verschiedenen Aufgabenformate.

Vor jeder Aufgabe steht ein Kreis ◯. Nimm dir nach dem Bearbeiten der Aufgabe Zeit, den Kreis auszumalen.

● Das kannst du schon gut: Prima!

● Das fällt dir noch schwer.
Tipp: Lies dir die passenden Inhalte im TB und im WB nochmals durch und wiederhole die Übung.

● Übe die Inhalte nochmals intensiv! Im TB findest du ab Seite 176 Grammatikerklärungen, ab Seite 201 Vokabellisten.

Vergiss nicht, deine Fortschritte immer in deinen Lernplan auf Seite 4 bis 5 einzutragen.

Diese Symbole kennst du bereits aus dem TB:

☆ leichte Aufgabe
☾ mittelschwere Aufgabe
☼ schwierige Aufgabe

Du kannst selbst entscheiden, mit welchem Schwierigkeitsgrad du beginnen möchtest. Du kannst zum Beispiel mit der ☆ Aufgabe anfangen und anschließend mit ☾ und ☼ intensiver üben. Trau dir ruhig auch schwierigere Übungen zu! Überprüfe deine Antworten mit dem Lösungsteil (ab Seite 106).

Jede Klassenarbeit beginnt mit Aufgaben zum **Hörverstehen**. Höre dazu die beiliegende CD. Als Hilfe findest du die Texte dazu im Anhang (Seite 124).

Lies jeden Text ganz genau und **unterstreiche** wichtige Informationen.

Schreibe einen Text. Vergiss nicht, deine **Antworttexte** sorgfältig zu **überprüfen**.

Wiederhole die **Vokabeln** gründlich und **regelmäßig**. Bei einigen Aufgaben werden dir neue Wörter in Fußnoten erklärt.

Wiederhole die wichtigen Grammatikregeln im TB ab Seite 176.

Übertrage nur die gefragten **Informationen** von einer Sprache in die andere.

Die **Sprechaufgaben** sind Einzel- und Partneraufgaben. Übe immer mit einem Partner (z. B. Eltern, Freunde)! Dein Partner kann dir **Rückmeldung** geben, ob dein Gesagtes richtig war und was du noch verbessern kannst. Du kannst dich aber auch aufnehmen und die Aufnahme einem Partner vorspielen.

! Übe vor jeder Klassenarbeit besonders die Aufgaben, die beim ersten Bearbeiten einen ● bekommen haben.

Tipps für die Klassenarbeit

Lies die **Arbeitsanweisungen** zu jeder Aufgabe ganz **genau durch**!
Wenn du trotz genauen Lesens eine Anweisung nicht verstehst, frage deine(n) Englischlehrer(in).

☑ Achte darauf, dass du **immer** eine Antwort ankreuzt! Wenn du gar nichts ankreuzt, bekommst du überhaupt keine Punkte. Aber selbst wenn du raten musst, hast du eine gute Chance, die richtige Antwort auszuwählen.

Viel Spaß beim Üben mit dem Klassenarbeitstrainer!

Inhalt und Lernplan

Plane die Arbeit mit dem Klassenarbeitstrainer und **überprüfe** deine Ergebnisse: Gleiche jeden Abschnitt, z. B. *Listening*, *Reading*, sorgfältig mit dem Lösungsheft ab. Trage ein, wann du die Seiten bearbeitet hast und notiere in der Ampel, wie dir die Übungen gelungen sind.

bearbeitet am

bearbeitet am

LISTENING

Tipp

Schritt 1 – **Vor dem ersten Hören:** Lies die Aufgabe(n).
Schritt 2 – **Beim ersten Hören:** Bearbeite die Aufgabe(n).
Schritt 3 – **Beim zweiten Hören:** Vervollständige und verbessere deine Antworten.

Let's talk about food

a) Rachel is in New York City to interview people for a school project. What is the project about? Listen to the interview and tick ✓ the correct answer.

The school project is about …

- ☐ the best restaurants in New York.
- ☐ the eating habits of New York teenagers.
- ☐ typical American food.

b) What did Karen, Jacques and Dennis have for breakfast (B), lunch (L) and dinner (D) yesterday? Listen again and write the letters in the correct boxes.

Karen	☐ cornflakes	☐ French fries	☐ rice with vegetables
	☐ a salad	☐ a vegetarian curry	
Jacques	☐ a bagel	☐ chili con carne	☐ Chinese food
	☐ a hamburger	☐ a turkey sandwich	
Dennis	☐ a cheese sandwich	☐ eggs and bacon	☐ pancakes
	☐ pasta with cheese	☐ pizza	

c) Read the sentence beginnings and endings. Listen again and tick ✓ the correct endings.

1. Karen thinks typical American food is …

A ☐ burger and French fries.
B ☐ sandwiches with salad.
C ☐ steak with potatoes.

2. Karen likes the farmers' market because …

A ☐ her best friend works there.
B ☐ it's on her way to work.
C ☐ the food is fresh and organic.

3. Jacques is a tourist from …

A ☐ Berlin.
B ☐ London.
C ☐ Paris.

4. Jacques and his friends had dinner …

A ☐ at a small restaurant.
B ☐ in their hotel room.
C ☐ near Times Square.

5. Dennis likes fast food because …

A ☐ it doesn't cost a lot of money.

B ☐ it helps him concentrate at school.

C ☐ there is no need to spend time cooking.

6. Dennis thinks he's healthy enough because …

A ☐ he does a lot of sports.

B ☐ he eats a lot of fruit.

C ☐ he often eats at home.

d) Answer the questions in complete sentences.

1. Why doesn't Karen like fast food?

____

____

____

2. Why does Karen cook her own dinner every day?

____

____

3. What is typical American food in Jacques's opinion? (three things)

____

____

4. What does Jacques think is special about food in New York?

____

____

5. How does Dennis's mother feel about breakfast?

____

____

6. What traditional American dishes does Dennis's mother make?

____

____

____

____

READING

Tipp

Schritt 1 – **Vor dem Lesen:** Sieh dir die **Überschrift** an und überlege, worum es gehen könnte. Lies die Aufgabe(n) und überlege, was gesucht ist.

Schritt 2 – **Beim Lesen: Unterstreiche** die Informationen, die für die Aufgabe(n) gesucht werden.

Secret sights in New York City

Read the text about secret sights in New York City.

Every tourist who comes to New York City wants to see its most famous sights: the Statue of Liberty, the Empire State Building, Brooklyn Bridge, Central Park and Ground Zero. What many people don't know is that there are many interesting "hidden"[1] sights in Manhattan – and some of them are really special!

A On Roosevelt Island in the East River between Manhattan and Queens, you'll find the Smallpox[2] Hospital[3]. It was built away from the city center to take care of people with smallpox – an illness that isn't a problem anymore today, but that killed many people all over the world. Many cities built special hospitals to keep the illness as far away from healthy people as possible. Between 1856 and 1875, about 7,000 patients came to the hospital every year. Today, you can take the bus to see the old building.

B Built in 1967, this might be just another office building – but it's actually a tropical garden. Trees and flowers grow inside the building and make their way down to a number of water pools. Glass walls make sure that the temperatures are just high enough for the plants to grow all year round. This building on East 43rd Street is surely one of the most unusual sights in Manhattan, and it is open to visitors all year round.

C A garbage[4] collection worker in New York City, Nelson Molina, started collecting little treasures[5] from the garbage about 25 years ago. His idea was simply to make his corner of the garage at work a little prettier. Soon, some of the other workers began adding little pieces. Everything is carefully chosen from the garbage of Manhattan, and everything has to be checked by Molina before it becomes part of the collection. The pieces are grouped by size and color. Come and take a very different look at New York City!

D Chris "Freedom" Pape, a graffiti artist, first came to the Amtrak tunnel in 1974 and started spray painting. The tunnel was built in the 1930s, but closed in 1980. A little later, homeless[6] people began to live there, and more street artists came to paint the tunnel walls. The Freedom Tunnel, as it is now called, is famous for its many different works of art. If you want to see the paintings, you can take a special train tour.

1 *hidden* ['hɪdn]: versteckt
2 *smallpox* ['smɔːlpɒks]: Pocken
3 *hospital* ['hɒspɪtl]: Krankenhaus
4 *garbage (AE)* ['gɑːrbɪdʒ]: Müll
5 *treasure* ['treʒə(r)]: Schatz
6 *homeless* ['həʊmləs]: obdachlos

☆ ☾ ☼ a) **Match each heading to the correct part of the text. There are more headings than you need.**

A building with a history • A special place to look at pictures • A garden in the city • A special book collection • The glass hotel • Treasures from the garbage

A ______

B ______

C ______

D ______

b) **Read the sentences and tick ✓ right or wrong.**

	right	wrong
1. Smallpox was a dangerous[1] illness.	☐	☐
2. About 7,000 patients came to the hospital between 1856 and 1875.	☐	☐
3. The tropical garden is in a Manhattan office building on East 43rd Street.	☐	☐
4. There are glass walls to make the building warm enough for the plants.	☐	☐
5. Only Nelson Molina decides what goes into the garbage collection.	☐	☐
6. Molina's garbage "museum" is organized by topic.	☐	☐
7. Street art in the Freedom Tunnel began in 1980.	☐	☐
8. You can take a tour of the Freedom Tunnel by train.	☐	☐

1 *dangerous* [ˈdeɪndʒərəs]: gefährlich

☾ ☼ c) **Correct the wrong sentences from b).**

______

______

______

______

______

______

______

______

______

d) Answer the questions in complete sentences.

1. Where is Roosevelt Island?

2. Why was the smallpox hospital built outside the city?

3. How can you get to the old hospital building on Roosevelt Island?

4. When can you visit the tropical garden on East 43rd Street?

5. How did Nelson Molina's collection start?

6. Who finds the pieces in Molina's garbage collection?

7. What happened after the Amtrak tunnel was closed?

WRITING

Tipp

Schritt 1 – **Vor dem Schreiben:** Prüfe, ob der Text eine bestimmte Form haben muss (z. B. E-Mail). Lege den Inhalt und die Reihenfolge fest.
Schritt 2 – **Schreibe** deinen Text.
Schritt 3 – **Überarbeite** deinen Text: Kontrolliere zuerst, ob alle Inhalte vorkommen. Prüfe dann, ob es Grammatik- oder Rechtschreibfehler gibt. Verbessere sie.

My neighbourhood

☆ **Write a short text about where you live. Describe your home town, your house or flat, and your neighbourhood. Explain what you (don't) like about where you live. Write about 80 words. The words and phrases in the boxes will help you.**

I live in … • It's a … town/city. • I live in a flat/house with … • We live near … • My neighbourhood is … • I (don't) like the fact that … • I think … is … • My favourite place is …

beautiful • big • boring • interesting • lively • pretty • nice • small • …

Start like this: I live in …

A travel guide

Write a short travel guide for your home town. Think about sights, activities for families, and places to eat and drink. Write about 100 words. The phrases in the box will help you. Make notes first.

You really must visit … • Our most famous sight is … • If you're interested in … you should … • Families love (going to) … • Enjoy your breakfast at … • We recommend … • …

- __________
- __________
- __________
- __________
- __________

A day in …

A day in New York City

You are visiting New York City with your best friend and his/her family. After a long and interesting day, you want to write an email to your parents about all the great sights you have seen. Write about 120 words. The ideas in the box will help you. Make notes first.

5th Avenue • Central Park • Ellis Island • Empire State Building • Flatiron Building • One World Trade Center • Statue of Liberty • Times Square • …

- ______________________
- ______________________
- ______________________
- ______________________
- ______________________

Start like this: Dear Mum and Dad,

What a day! …

MEDIATION

Tipp

Gib in deinen eigenen Worten die **wichtigen Informationen** in der jeweils **anderen Sprache** wieder. Du musst **nicht Wort für Wort** übersetzen! Passe dabei deine Ausdrucksweise der Situation und den Sprecherinnen und Sprechern an.

○ Holiday food in the USA

You are staying with an American family in Pennsylvania for a year. Your mother is visiting for Christmas, but her English is not very good. Help out at the dinner table.

Mother: Was essen denn Amerikaner normalerweise zu Weihnachten?

You: My mum would like to know ______________________________

____

Cathy: Well, we usually eat turkey on Thanksgiving and at Christmas. For dessert we often have some kind of pie like apple or pumpkin pie.

You: Sie essen zum Erntedankfest und ______________________________

____

____

Robert: What do you eat at Christmas in Germany?

You: Robert möchte wissen, was ______________________________

____

Mother: Wir essen gern Fisch zu Weihnachten, aber viele Familien essen Kartoffelsalat und Würstchen. Es gibt kein Gericht, das alle Deutschen zu Weihnachten essen.

You: We like to eat ______________________________

____

____

Mother: Was essen sie denn als Beilage zum Truthahn?

You: She asks what ______________________________

Robert: Usually we have vegetables like broccoli, carrots or beans, and of course potatoes.

You: Es gibt ______________________________

____

Mother: Alles schmeckt sehr lecker! Aber warum sind die Kartoffeln orange?

You: My mum says ______________________________

She would like to know ______________________________

Robert: These aren't normal potatoes – they're sweet potatoes[1]. We often eat them on special days.

You: Robert sagt, dass ______________________________

____

Mother: Ich weiß gar nicht, was Amerikaner normalerweise essen. Ich kenne nur Hamburger und Hot Dogs.

You: She says that she doesn't ______________________________

____

Cathy: Well, I like salad. The kids love fruit, so we often go to the farmers' market to buy fresh fruit and vegetables.

You: Cathy isst gern ______________________________

____

Robert: I like fast food or traditional dishes like meat loaf. Cathy wants me to eat healthy food, so we don't eat hamburgers or hot dogs very often.

You: Robert mag ______________________________

aber Cathy möchte, ______________________________

Mother: In Deutschland sind italienische oder chinesische Restaurants sehr beliebt. Wie ist das hier?

You: In Germany, ______________________________

What about ______________________________

Cathy: There are lots of different restaurants here. We like Italian, Mexican and Chinese food.

You: Cathy sagt, dass ______________________________

____

Mother: Das Essen war wunderbar. Ich möchte morgen gern ein deutsches Gericht für Sie kochen.

You: She says that ______________________________

1 *sweet potato*: Süßkartoffel

WORDS AND GRAMMAR

Words, words, words

Tipp

Streiche die Wörter, die du bereits verwendet hast, in der Box **durch**. So behältst du leichter den Überblick.

Read the definitions. What is it? Use the words in the box. There is one more word than you need.

skill • south • culture • capital • step • impression • settler

1. the most important town or city of a country: ______
2. a person who goes to live in a new country that doesn't have many inhabitants: ______
3. several of these take you from one floor of a building to another: ______
4. something that you can do well: ______
5. an idea or feeling about somebody you have just met: ______
6. one of the four directions – north, east, west and: ______

Complete the sentences with the correct words. Be careful to use the correct form.

1. The USA has fifty s _ _ _ _ _, for example New York, California and Florida.
2. Many people live in the USA – it has over 300 million i _ _ _ _ _ _ _ _ _ _ _ _ _.
3. The Empire State Building is very tall – it has 102 f _ _ _ _ _ _.
4. The city centres are always b _ _ _ at weekends.
5. People in the USA speak different l _ _ _ _ _ _ _ _. Most speak English or Spanish.

6. Have you read the r _ _ _ _ _ of the new James Bond film? It must be really good!
7. I live in a small f _ _ _ on the third floor.
8. Can you i _ _ _ _ _ _ _ winning a million dollars? I would buy a new car.

Choose six words from the box and write definitions for them.

background • centre • community • complain • enjoy oneself • fact file • immigrant • study

1. ______________________________
____
2. ______________________________
____

3. ______________________________
4. ______________________________
5. ______________________________
6. ______________________________

Phrases

Match the parts to complete the phrases.

A	contact
B	good
C	enjoy
D	traditional
E	write
F	complain

1	impression
2	centre
3	a friend
4	a review
5	about something
6	dish
7	yourself

A	
B	
C	
D	
E	
F	

Complete the phrases with the words from the box. There is one more word than you need.

take place • immigrant • skill • support • busy • presentation • flat • floor • imagine

1. learn a new ______________ for life
2. give a history ______________
3. be a new ______________
4. live in a big ______________
5. ______________ a sports team
6. a ______________ city centre
7. ______________ on Wednesday afternoon
8. ______________ an exciting story

American English

Find eight words from Theme 1 that belong to American English (AE).

American English

Reflexive pronouns

a) Match the reflexive pronouns from the box to the correct personal pronouns.

Tipp

Du verwendest Reflexivpronomen, wenn das Subjekt und das Objekt in einem Satz dieselbe Person bezeichnen: **Billy** took a picture of himself in front of the Empire State Building.

yourselves • himself • myself • ourselves • yourself • itself • themselves • herself

Singular	Plural
I →	we →
you →	you →
he →	they →
she →	
it →	

b) Read the sentences and circle the correct reflexive pronoun.

1. Tom, look at **yourself / itself**! Your face is dirty!
2. I can't look at **myself / yourself**. I hate my new haircut.
3. Our football team has won! The players should be proud of **himself / themselves**.
4. Sarah is really nervous about the test on Friday. She should believe in **itself / herself**.
5. I have to take a look at my bike this weekend. It's not going to repair **myself / itself**!
6. I am sure you will enjoy **yourselves / ourselves** at the match.

Complete the sentences with the correct reflexive pronouns from the box. There is one more pronoun than you need and you will have to use one of the pronouns twice.

myself • yourself • himself • herself • ourselves • yourselves • themselves

1. My finger hurts a little. I cut ________________ with a knife earlier.
2. Sam and Tom, you should believe in ________________. I'm sure you'll win.
3. They didn't collect the money for ________________ – it was for a charity.
4. Our dog can look after ________________ for a few hours. He'll probably just sleep.
5. I sometimes talk to ________________ when my homework is difficult.
6. Our holiday was great! We really enjoyed ________________.
7. Jane taught ________________ a bit of Spanish before her trip.

Complete the sentences. Decide whether you need a word from the orange box or the blue box.

me • you • him • her • us	myself • himself • herself • itself • ourselves • themselves

1. "My computer keeps turning ________________ off. I don't know what's wrong."

– "Don't worry, I'll help ________________. I'm sure we can repair it together."

2. Annie hurt ________________ when she cleaned the windows.

Luckily her sister was there to help ________________.

3. Excuse me, we're lost. Could you please tell ________________ how to get to the Empire State Building?
4. Zachary is good at maths, but he needs to believe in ________________ more.

I think you should talk to ________________.

5. I'm rather angry with ________________. I forgot to return some books to the library yesterday.
6. Mum, we're old enough to look after ________________ at home. Have fun at the cinema!
7. Tara and Alan are really enjoying ________________ in New York.

I know because they called ________________ yesterday.

Shopping for clothes

Kevin's mother takes him shopping for new clothes. Complete the dialogue with 'one' or 'ones'.

Mother: OK, let's start. What about a sweater – do you need a new ____________?

Kevin: I guess I do. But I don't like these white sweaters here – I prefer dark ____________.

Mother: Here are some grey sweaters … and there are some blue ____________ over there.

Kevin: Can I have a dark blue ____________?

Mother: Sure! Try this ____________ on. It's a large.

Kevin: I think that's the right size. Hey, there are some cool sweaters in that corner!

Mother: What, the ____________ by the door? They're really expensive – £65!

Pete needs new clothes. Cross out the repeated nouns and use 'one' or 'ones' instead.

Father: We really need to buy some new clothes for you. The ~~clothes~~ ones you have are too small now. Let's see. There are a lot of shops to choose from. This <u>shop</u> looks interesting.

Pete: OK.

Father: Wonderful! Come on. You need some new T-shirts. Your old <u>T-shirts</u> look terrible.

Pete: I like the <u>T-shirts</u> in that corner over there.

Father: Try them on, then. OK, jackets are over there. Would you like a blue <u>jacket</u> or a black <u>jacket</u>?

Pete: I'd prefer green.

Father: Well, you can try this <u>jacket</u> on then. Look, there are some pullovers by the window. I think you could use some new <u>pullovers</u>.

Pete: I don't like the <u>pullovers</u> they have here. Let's try a different shop.

☼ **Lelaina needs new clothes. Cross out the repeated nouns and use 'one' or 'ones' instead.**

Lelaina: I think I need some new shoes. All my old ~~shoes~~ ones don't look good anymore.

Mother: What about the shoes you bought last month?

Lelaina: I don't like them anymore. They make my feet hurt.

Mother: Well, OK. What about dresses?

Lelaina: I saw some nice dresses in a shop down the road.

Mother: What about this dress right here? Look, it's your size.

Lelaina: I don't really like the colour. But I'd also like a new skirt. Have you seen the skirt that Annie bought last week? It looks fantastic!

Mother: No, I haven't. Why don't you try this skirt on?

Lelaina: I prefer the skirts in the shop next door. They've also got cool scarves. I want to look at the scarf in the shop window. Annie has got the same scarf.

Mother: OK, I give up. Let's go next door then.

○ Some or any?

Tipp

Du verwendest *some* und seine Zusammensetzungen in **bejahten Aussagesätzen**.
In **verneinten Aussagen** und **Fragen** verwendest du *any* und seine Zusammensetzungen.
Achtung: Wenn man um etwas bittet oder etwas anbietet, benutzt man *some* auch in Fragen.

☆ **Read the sentences and circle the correct words.**

1. Mum, can you give me **any / some** money? I need it for lunch.
2. Zach can't find his jacket **anywhere / somewhere**. He must have left it at school.
3. I'm sorry, but we can't have pancakes – I haven't got **any / some** eggs.
4. John, can you come over here? I think I saw **anyone / someone** in the garden.
5. It's Fiona's birthday next week, but I can't think of **anything / something** to get her.
6. Sarah, you haven't had a real holiday in a long time. You should go **anywhere / somewhere** nice this summer.

Complete the sentences with the words from the box.

- some
- somebody
- something
- somewhere
- any
- anybody
- anything
- anywhere

1. There are ______________ interesting articles in today's newspaper.
2. I can't find my sandwich. I'm sure ______________ has eaten it.
3. Has ______________ seen Dave today? Is he ill?
4. Mum, I want to go to the party tomorrow, but I haven't got ______________ to wear!
5. Can we go to Washington, D.C. next weekend? I haven't been ______________ this year yet.

6. Welcome, Mrs Henderson! Would you like ______________ to drink?
7. I don't know what to do on my birthday. I really haven't got ______________ ideas.
8. Lucy must be ______________ around here. I saw her only a minute ago.

Complete the sentences with the words from the box. There is one more word than you need, and you have to use one word twice.

any • somebody • something • anywhere • anything • some • anybody • somewhere

1. Can you help me? I think there's ______________ in my left eye.
2. Julie, there's ______________ at the door. Can you go and look, please?
3. Justin is new in town – he doesn't really know ______________ yet.
4. Do you live ______________ near Sandy? Somebody should take her today's homework.
5. It's really hot in here. I need ______________ to drink.
6. Do you know if Frank is ill? – Sorry, but I don't know ______________ about why he isn't here.
7. I really like fruit, but I can't find ______________ apples.
8. Look in the kitchen. I think you will find ______________ there.

SPEAKING

My favourite sports

Tipp

Schritt 1 – Überlege, was du sagen möchtest und **welche Worte** du dafür benötigst.
Schritt 2 – Sprich in **ganzen Sätzen**. Umschreibe Worte, die dir nicht einfallen, **auf Englisch**.

Read the texts and talk about sports. You can also add other sports.

- What is your favourite sport?
- How do you do/play it?
- When and where do you do/play it?

- Who do you do/play it with?
- Which sport do you like to try?

Lacrosse: A team sport played with a lacrosse stick and ball. The head of the stick is used to catch, carry and shoot the ball into the goal. There are ten players in each team.

Baseball: A ball game between two teams of nine players each. One player throws the ball and another tries to hit it with a stick (the 'bat'). The second player must then try to run around the field once before the other team has the ball.

Swimming: Races are held in four different styles, with freestyle being the fastest. Swimming just for fun is one of the most popular sports, and also one of the healthiest.

Field Hockey: A ball game between two teams of eleven players. A wooden stick is used to hit the ball and score a goal. Only the flat side of the stick may be used.

Answer three of the questions and give reasons. The phrases in the box will help you.

My favourite sport is … because … • I like … because … • I think … is cool/… because … • You need a lacrosse/baseball/hockey field/pool. • You need … to do/play it. • There are … players in each team. • I do/play/go … every Monday/… at 5 pm/6 pm/… • I would (really) like to try … because … • I think … would be fun/exciting/interesting/…

Answer four of the questions and give reasons. The phrases in the box will help you.

My favourite sport is … • I like … • I think … You need … • There are … in each team. • I do/play/go every … at … I would (really) like to try … • I think … would be …

Answer all of the questions and give reasons.

LISTENING

Tipp

Schritt 1 – **Vor dem ersten Hören:** Lies die Aufgabe(n).
Schritt 2 – **Beim ersten Hören:** Bearbeite die Aufgabe(n).
Schritt 3 – **Beim zweiten Hören:** Vervollständige und verbessere deine Antworten.

○ My biggest challenge

a) Listen to Tom, Jenny, Pamela and James talking about challenges in their lives. Then write the correct name under each picture. There are two more pictures than you need.

1

____

2

____

3

____

4

____

5

____

6

____

b) Listen again and tick ✓ right or wrong.

	right	wrong
1. Tom and his parents have a farm with lots of animals.	☐	☐
2. Tom's dad is looking for a new job at the moment.	☐	☐
3. Jenny's grandmother can't go to the supermarket.	☐	☐
4. Jenny goes shopping for her grandmother twice a week.	☐	☐
5. Pamela stands on a chair when she hangs a picture.	☐	☐
6. She works on her problem with a group of other people.	☐	☐
7. James's family helped him quit smoking.	☐	☐
8. James really wants to smoke another cigarette.	☐	☐

c) Correct the wrong sentences from b).

d) Answer the questions in complete sentences.

1. Why do people love the vegetables that Tom's family sells?

2. Why is Tom proud of his father?

3. Where does Jenny's grandmother live?

4. What is Jenny's grandmother happy about?

5. How did Pamela feel after dealing with her challenge?

6. When did James quit smoking?

7. Why did James start smoking when he was younger?

READING

Tipp

Schritt 1 – **Vor dem Lesen:** Sieh dir die **Überschrift** an und überlege, worum es gehen könnte. Lies die Aufgabe(n) und überlege, was gesucht ist.

Schritt 2 – **Beim Lesen: Unterstreiche** die Informationen, die für die Aufgabe(n) gesucht werden.

Working hard makes winning feel better

Read the text about Janet's big challenge.

Hi everybody,

My name is Janet and I'd like to tell you about a big challenge in my life.

When I was six years old, I started doing track and field[1]. I loved it and I was a very good athlete – I won a lot of races and competitions. Training was three or four times a week, even in snow or bad weather. Every year I got a little better and my parents were very proud of me. There were articles about me in the local newspaper. I wasn't really famous, but people in my home town knew who I was.

When I was 16, I took part in a heptathlon. That is a competition with seven different events in two days, for example a 200-metre race and a high jump. My best friend Kelly also took part – in some events I was first, and in other events she was. In the end, I lost to her by six points. She was happy about winning, of course, but I was really sad and I had a hard time. Some of our friends even made fun of me a little and said, "Do you want me to give you six points?" I did not want to lose like that again.

I decided to train even harder, but six weeks later, I broke my leg playing basketball. I had to stay in hospital[2] for ten days. Competitions that year were over for me. My friends all came to visit me, but they made me angry because they were fit and I had an injury.

I found it really hard to deal with my injury. Sport was my life and I loved running and training. Now, I had to start all over again. I was sad for a little while, but my family and friends supported me a lot and with their help, I managed to turn things around. As soon as I could use my leg again, my parents went for a walk in the park with me every day. Kelly was always there for me and went swimming with me to help my leg get strong again.

In the spring, I started training again and it felt wonderful to be back. I had to start slowly, but after about two months, I was able to run and jump three or four times a week again. In May, I was taking part in competitions. That year was my best one yet! I won lots of competitions, even against my best friend Kelly. Sometimes she won, but that was OK for me now.

Dealing with this challenge taught me a lot about myself. For the first time, I had to work really hard to do well in competitions, and that made winning feel even better! That experience has actually helped me because I have learned not to give up.

1 *track and field* [ˌtræk æn ˈfiːld]: Leichtathletik
2 *hospital* [ˈhɒspɪtl]: Krankenhaus

a) **Look at the heading. What does Janet mean when she says "Working hard makes winning feel better"? Tick ✓ the correct answer.**

- ☐ Being successful feels even better when you've had to work for it.
- ☐ If you work hard before a competition, you can win.
- ☐ With the support of your family and friends, you can do anything.

b) **Read the sentences and tick ✓ right or wrong.**

	right	wrong
1. Janet has been doing track and field since she was sixteen.	☐	☐
2. She practised several times a week in any weather.	☐	☐
3. Janet was a famous athlete in her home town.	☐	☐
4. There are seven events in heptathlon and a competition takes two days.	☐	☐
5. In one event, Janet lost to her best friend Kelly by six points.	☐	☐
6. Janet broke her arm a month later when she was playing basketball.	☐	☐
7. She had to stay in hospital for six weeks.	☐	☐
8. After her injury, she started training again in the spring.	☐	☐
9. Janet's first competition after her injury was in May.	☐	☐
10. Janet was very successful in the year following her injury.	☐	☐

c) **Correct the wrong sentences from b).**

___

___

___

___

___

___

___

___

___

___

___

___

d) Answer the questions in complete sentences.

1. How did people in Janet's home town know who she was?

2. How did Janet feel about losing to Kelly by only a few points?

3. Why was Janet angry when her friends visited her in hospital?

4. How did Janet's parents help her after her injury?

5. What did Kelly do for Janet after her injury?

6. How long was it after Janet started training again that she was able to train as often as before?

7. How does Janet feel now when Kelly wins competitions?

8. What has this experience taught Janet for later life?

WRITING

Tipp

Schritt 1 – **Vor dem Schreiben:** Prüfe, ob der Text eine bestimmte Form haben muss (z. B. E-Mail). Lege den Inhalt und die Reihenfolge fest.
Schritt 2 – **Schreibe** deinen Text.
Schritt 3 – **Überarbeite** deinen Text: Kontrolliere zuerst, ob alle Inhalte vorkommen. Prüfe dann, ob es Grammatik- oder Rechtschreibfehler gibt. Verbessere sie.

◯ Halima's biggest challenge

☆ **Look at the pictures. What was Halima's biggest challenge? Tell her story in about 80 words. The phrases in the box will help you.**

1

3

2

4

start smoking • be part of the group • feel stressed and unhealthy • parents angry • want me to quit • try to quit • need support • join a support group • help each other • don't smoke anymore • feel happy and healthy

Start like this: When I was 14 years old, I started smoking. ...

Christopher's biggest challenge

Christopher has just dealt with a big challenge: he finished a 10-kilometre sponsored run to raise money for a charity. Write about his experience. Think about the following questions:

- What was difficult about the challenge?
- How did he deal with the challenge?
- How did he feel afterwards?

Write about 100 words. The phrases in the box will help you.

(don't) enjoy running • get fit • train with a friend • go running several times a week • friends/family agree to give money • (manage to) finish the race • feel proud/tired/happy/…

Start like this: My biggest challenge was …

Their biggest challenge

Look at the pictures and choose one. Write about that person's biggest challenge. Think about the following questions:

- What was the person's challenge?
- How did it start?
- How did he/she feel?

- What was difficult about the challenge?
- Who or what helped the person?
- What is the situation now?

Write about 120 words. The ideas in the boxes will help you.

Susan took care of her grandparents

Charlie raised money for children who are ill

Anne stood up to someone who bullied a younger child

break an arm/leg • help after school • cook/clean/shop/…	children's hospital[1] • organize a charity event • friends/family help	take a child's lunch money • too scared to tell anyone • get the child's money back

1 *hospital* ['hɒspɪtl]: Krankenhaus

Start like this: My biggest challenge was ...

MEDIATION

Tipp

Gib in deinen eigenen Worten die **wichtigen Informationen** in der jeweils **anderen Sprache** wieder. Du musst **nicht Wort für Wort** übersetzen! Passe dabei deine Ausdrucksweise der Situation und den Sprecherinnen und Sprechern an.

A support group

Samantha wants to quit smoking, so she has joined a support group for smokers. When her Uncle Hartmut, who is German, visits her in Chicago, he comes along to the group. Hartmut's English is not very good, so Samantha has to help out.

Samantha: Hello everybody! This is my Uncle Hartmut. He's from Germany.

Phil: Welcome, Hartmut! I'm Phil. Are you in America to visit Samantha?

Samantha: Das ist Phil. Er fragt, ______________________________

____

Hartmut: Ja, ich besuche Samanthas Familie. Ihre Mutter ist meine Schwester.

Samantha: Hartmut says that ______________________________

____

Hartmut: Samantha hat mir von der Gruppe erzählt. Ich möchte auch gern etwas verändern und mit dem Rauchen aufhören.

Samantha: He says that I ______________________________

____

Jack: I know what you mean. My girlfriend was really angry with me, too, because all my clothes always smelled of cigarette smoke.

Samantha: Jack erzählt, dass seine Freundin ______________________________

____

____

Alison: I think going to a support group is the right thing to do. It has really helped me.

Samantha: Das ist Alison. Sie findet, ______________________________

____

____

Hartmut: Das ist gut. Ich bin immer müde und habe keine Energie.

Samantha: He says that ______________________________

____

Hartmut: Wie habt ihr denn mit dem Rauchen aufgehört?

Samantha: Hartmut would like to know ______________________________

Alison: I tried smoking less – 20 cigarettes in the first week, ten in the second. I also used nicotine gum.

Samantha: Alison sagt, dass sie ______________________________

____

____

Phil: I was really tired at first and I always wanted to smoke a cigarette. But after a few weeks, I was already fitter. I could run for longer and I did more fun activities.

Samantha: Phil erzählt, dass er ______________________________

____

____

Hartmut: Das klingt gut. Ich sollte wirklich mehr Sport machen. Ich gehe zum Beispiel gerne schwimmen.

Samantha: Hartmut thinks ______________________________

____

____

Jack: Many people gain a little weight when they quit smoking. It helps to eat healthy food. I enjoy trying new recipes.

Samantha: Jack erzählt, dass ______________________________

____

____

Hartmut: Danke, das werde ich versuchen. Ich glaube, ich suche mir zu Hause auch eine Gruppe. Ich bin sicher, es ist einfacher, wenn man sich gegenseitig unterstützt.

Samantha: Hartmut says ______________________________

____

WORDS AND GRAMMAR

Phrases

Match the parts to complete the phrases.

A	face
B	smoke
C	test
D	quit
E	have
F	know

1	a lot of energy
2	your rights and responsibilities
3	a personal challenge
4	a new century
5	a cigarette
6	somebody's courage
7	smoking

A	
B	
C	
D	
E	
F	

a) Complete the phrases with the words from the box. There is one more word than you need.

seem • test • face • be proud of • leave • get • climb • advise • hurt

1. ____________ a difficult problem
2. ____________ a high mountain
3. ____________ winning a race
4. ____________ a friend to quit smoking
5. ____________ angry quickly
6. ____________ like a nice person
7. ____________ yourself in an accident
8. ____________ rubbish around

b) Use the phrases from a) to write sentences.

____

____

____

____

____

____

____

____

____

Crosswords

☆ **Complete the crossword puzzle and find the solution word.**

1. Clara has decided to … a high mountain.
2. Every time you smoke a …, it is bad for your health.
3. You … happy. Did your maths test go well?
4. If you stay outside in the sun too long, it will burn your … .
5. People who quit smoking often have a lot more … . They feel much fitter.
6. My grandmother does her shopping at the local … . They've got everything she needs.

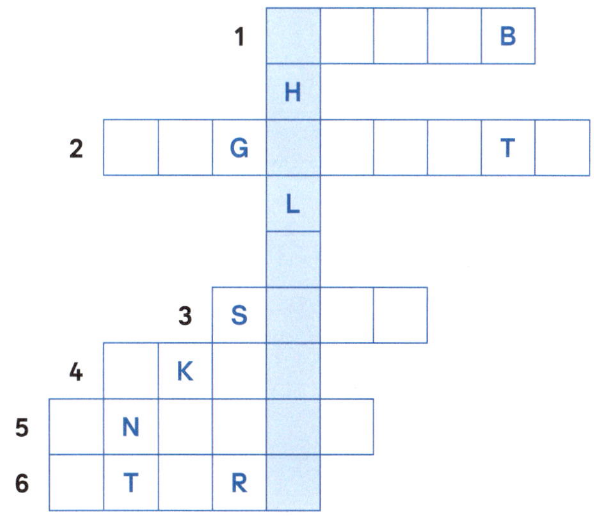

Solution word:

	H		L					

☾ **Complete the crossword puzzle.**

1. If you …, your clothes and hair will smell of cigarettes.
2. If you … something, it means that you have to deal with it.
3. Sometimes you need a lot of … to deal with a difficult challenge.
4. A … helpline is there to help young people with any problem they have.
5. After climbing for three hours, we made it to the … of the mountain.
6. If you think somebody is nice to look at, you find him/her … .
7. Children everywhere in the world should have the … to go to school.

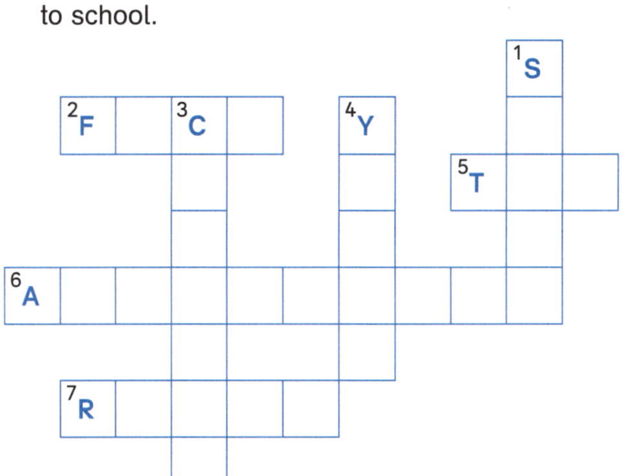

Explain

What do the following words mean? Explain them in English.

1. resident: ______________________________

____

2. courage: ______________________________

____

3. to advise somebody: ______________________________

____

4. challenge: ______________________________

____

____

5. sheet: ______________________________

____

6. to remove: ______________________________

____

What do you enjoy doing?

Ben and Gail are talking about their hobbies. Complete the sentences with the -ing forms of the verbs in brackets () as nouns.

Ben: ___Playing___ (play) the guitar is my favourite activity. I love ______________ (practise) with my band. I think ______________ (be) in a band is really cool. All the girls love it!

Gail: I prefer sports. ______________ (swim) keeps me fit. I love ______________ (go) to the pool in the afternoon. Of course I always enjoy ______________ (win) competitions.

Ben: I think it's important to have a hobby, but ______________ (get) good marks at school is also important – even though I hate ______________ (do) my homework.

Ben and Gail are talking about what they like. Complete the sentences with the -ing forms of the verbs in the box as nouns. There is one more verb than you need.

relax • write • eat • visit • dance • spend • listen • get • try

Ben: I like ______________________ time with my band. We enjoy ______________________ songs together and I really like ______________________ different instruments.

Gail: My friends and I often meet after school. We enjoy just ______________________ in the park together or ______________________ to loud music. At weekends, we like to go ______________________ at the youth club together – they often have good parties there.

Ben: I like ______________________ my grandma on Sundays. ______________________ home-made waffles or cake is not a bad way to spend an afternoon!

Ben and Gail are talking about their everyday life. Write sentences about what they like, enjoy, are proud of etc. Use -ing forms as nouns.

Example: Gail: I hate getting up (hate / get up) at 6 am. I wish school didn't start so early.

Ben: I agree. I really ______________________ (not like / have) breakfast alone. My mum has to leave for work early, so I'm all by myself at breakfast time.

Gail: I have to say I really ______________________ (enjoy / walk) to school. When it's raining, I go by bus, but I ______________________ (hate / take) the bus. You never get a seat.

Ben: I know what you mean, but ______________________ (wait) in line at lunchtime is really bad, too. It takes forever to get your food.

Gail: You know, I just ______________________ (love / come) home to a nice cup of tea and some biscuits. My mum and I always talk a little before I do my homework.

Ben: That's really nice. My parents and I always cook dinner together. I think ______________________ (help) at home is important. ______________________ (tidy) the living room is my job.

Gail: I also have to help a little, but that's OK. I ______________________ (like / feed) the dog, for example.

Tell me what to do

Coach Miller talked to the American football team at high school before an important match, but Aidan was late and missed the talk. Report what the coach told the team (not) to do.

Example: "Warm up before the match."
Coach Miller told us to warm up before the match.

1. "Run as fast as possible with the ball."

Coach Miller told us to ______

2. "Watch the players on the other team."

He told us to ______

3. "Don't let the other team score too many points."

Coach Miller told us not to ______

4. "Drink lots of water during the breaks."

He told us ______

5. "Don't be late for the second half of the game."

He told us not ______

6. "Enjoy the game!"

He told us ______

Carole and Tina want to make a birthday cake for their best friend Sally. Carole's mother has told Carole what (not) to do. Report to Tina what she said. Use the verbs in brackets ().

Example: "Make a list of all the ingredients." (tell)
My mother told me to make a list of all the ingredients.

1. "Mix the butter and sugar in a big bowl." (tell)

My mother told me ______

2. "Add the eggs, flour and milk slowly." (tell)

______

3. "Don't bake the cake for more than 60 minutes." (advise)

She advised me not to ______

4. "Take the cake out and let it cool for an hour." (tell)

____

5. "Don't touch the hot oven[1]." (tell)

____

6. "Prepare some fresh cream for the cake." (tell)

____

7. "Put chocolate or fruit on top of the cream." (advise)

____

8. "Don't put the candles on the cake too soon." (advise)

____

1 *oven* ['ʌvn]: Backofen

These teenagers have to do little jobs around the house. Report what their parents and grandparents told or asked them (not) to do.

Example: Charles's grandmother: "Buy everything on my shopping list."

Charles's grandmother asked him to buy everything on her shopping list.

1. Melissa's father: "Please take out the rubbish."

Melissa's father asked her ____

2. Tim and Kathy's parents: "Tidy the living room."

____

3. Elena's mother: "Clean your rabbits' cage."

____

4. Zoe and Kyle's grandfather: "Please find my reading glasses for me."

____

____

5. David's father: "Don't leave your dirty plate on the table."

____

____

6. Anne and Henry's grandparents: "Please don't eat cake in your bedrooms."

____

____

____

7. Andy's parents: "Don't forget your grandmother's birthday."

____

____

____

____

8. Becca's mother: "Please repair your bike before school tomorrow."

____

____

____

What have you been doing?

Complete the sentences with the present perfect progressive of the verbs in brackets ().

Example: Jean has been trying (try) to call her best friend for about ten minutes.

1. Tom ______________________ (do) judo since he was eight years old.

2. I ______________________ (work) on my history presentation since 3 pm.

3. Richard ______________________ (wait) for his food for nearly an hour.

4. Jessica and her friends ______________________ (play) Monopoly for six hours.

5. You ______________________ (drive) for four hours. Let's take a break.

6. Jill and Rita's parents ______________________ (watch) them play for a while.

Complete the sentences with the present perfect progressive of the verbs in the box. There is one more verb than you need.

work • ~~wait~~ • not go out • take • practise • not learn • read • make • sleep • travel

Example: Barbara has been waiting for Tom for half an hour. He's always late!

1. Alex ______________________ all afternoon. Is he ill?

2. My grandfather ______________________ driving lessons since August.

3. Sally and Jonas ______________________ for long, but they're very happy together.

4. Dad ______________________ since this morning. His new book must be good.

5. Chris ______________________ for this concert for weeks. He's really good now.

6. Gerald ______________________ here since 2005. He likes his job.

7. Fred ______________________ German for long, but he's already quite good.

8. Sheila's grandparents ______________________ around the world for six months.

Complete the questions in the present perfect progressive and give short answers if needed.

Example: Has Emily been baking all morning? – Yes, she has. She wants the party to be perfect.

1. Have ______________________ (you / work) here for long?

– Yes, ______________________. For nearly ten years now.

2. ______________________ (Joe / sit) there since this morning?

– No, ______________________. He has just come in from the garden.

3. ______________________ (the children / watch) TV for long?

– No, ______________________. They have just come home from school.

4. ______________________ (Linda / help) you with your homework?

– Yes, ______________________. She has explained everything to me.

5. How long has Gemma ______________________ (Gemma / try) to repair her car?

– I'm not sure, but she seems to know what the problem is now.

6. What ______________________ (you / do) all morning?

– I have been in the park with some friends. Sorry, ______________________ (you / look) for me?

7. How long ______________________ (dad / tidy up) the house?
– For about three hours, but he's finished now. I feel bad – I should have helped him.

8. How long ______________________ (Jack / learn) for his maths test?
– For a week, I think. He should believe in himself more – I know he's good at maths.

The passive

Complete these passive sentences with the correct forms of the verbs in brackets ().

1. Karen has been ______________ (choose) to represent her school in the town championships. She is very proud.

2. Many different languages are ______________ (speak) in America.

3. Jim's car was ______________ (steal) in New York. He was very upset about it.

4. Land diving is ______________ (do) by young men on Vanuatu to show their courage.

5. The big tree in our garden is very old. It is going to be ______________ (cut) down by our gardener.

6. I would like to go to the football match, but all the tickets have been

______________ (sell).

Complete the sentences using the passive with 'was' or 'were'. Use the verbs in the box. There is one more verb than you need.

publish • make • get • build • take • feed • leave

1. These messages were ______________________ for you today. At least two are from grandma.

2. My grandparents' house ______________________ in 1997. It's very nice and quite modern.

3. The hamsters ______________________ an hour ago. They don't need any food now.

4. Natalie's birthday cake ______________________ by her best friends Ashley and Hannah.

5. These pictures ______________________ during our holiday in Peru. We had a great time there.

6. This book ______________________ last month. I think you'll like it – it's great!

Rewrite these sentences in the passive.

Example: Someone returned the red dress to the shop.
The red dress was returned to the shop.

1. Someone has sent Lydia some beautiful flowers.

Some beautiful flowers have been

2. The building manager will collect the rent next week.

3. Some pupils raised nearly £2,000 for a local charity last weekend.

4. Someone has sprayed graffiti on one of the school walls.

5. The men in the village build a tower for land diving every year.

6. People sell many different kinds of vegetable at the local farmers' market.

SPEAKING

Facing a challenge

Work with a partner. Look at the pictures on page 45.

a) Choose one of the pictures and have a conversation. A begins. The phrases in the boxes will help you.
b) Choose a different picture and swap roles. Have another conversation.

Partner A

Du bist die Person auf dem Foto. Du hast gerade eine schwierige Herausforderung geschafft.

Begrüße B und sage, dass du gerade eine schwierige Herausforderung geschafft hast.

Dann beantworte Bs Fragen.

Partner B

Die Person auf dem Foto ist dein/e Freund/in. Er/Sie hat gerade eine schwierige Herausforderung geschafft.

Begrüße A. Frage, …
- was die Herausforderung war.
- was daran schwierig war.
- wie sich A in der Situation gefühlt hat.
- wer/was A bei der Herausforderung geholfen hat.

Partner A
It was difficult because …
I (don't) like … • I'm (not) good at … • sad/alone/nervous/angry/scared/proud/tired … • My friends/family/… helped me.

Partner B
What was the …?
What was difficult about …?
How did you feel (about) …?
Who/What helped you to …?

- speak in front of the class
- prepare a good presentation
- practise with a friend

- need to be very fit
- practise with others
- take great pictures

- mother/father has a new job
- new school in a new city
- find new friends

- want to do something for other people
- hard work during the holidays
- made people very happy

- relationship not working
- difficult to tell him/her
- was right decision

- parents work a lot/ill/…
- prepare meals for the children/play with them

It was difficult because … • I (don't) like … • I'm (not) good at …

What was …? • How did you feel (about) …? • Who/What helped you …?

speak in front of … • be well prepared • practise

very fit • practise • great pictures

live in new town • new school • make friends

good/hard work • summer holidays • people happy

relationship not working • difficult • right decision

parents work a lot/ill/… prepare meals • play • proud

give a presentation in class

climb a high mountain

adapt to life in a new town

help build a house
for poor people

break up with a boyfriend
or girlfriend

take care of younger brothers
and sisters

a) Choose one of the pictures and have a conversation. A begins.
b) Choose a different picture and swap roles. Have another conversation.

Partner A

Du bist die Person auf dem Foto. Du hast gerade eine schwierige Herausforderung geschafft.

Begrüße B und sage, dass du gerade eine schwierige Herausforderung geschafft hast.

Dann beantworte Bs Fragen.

Partner B

Die Person auf dem Foto ist dein/e Freund/in. Er/Sie hat gerade eine schwierige Herausforderung geschafft.

Begrüße A. Frage, …
- was die Herausforderung war.
- was daran schwierig war.
- wie sich A in der Situation gefühlt hat.
- wer/was A bei der Herausforderung geholfen hat.
- wie sich A anschließend gefühlt hat.

LISTENING

Tipp

Schritt 1 – **Vor dem ersten Hören:** Lies die Aufgabe(n).
Schritt 2 – **Beim ersten Hören:** Bearbeite die Aufgabe(n).
Schritt 3 – **Beim zweiten Hören:** Vervollständige und verbessere deine Antworten.

West Side Story

a) Listen to Teresa talking about *West Side Story*. Where is she?

☐

☐

☐

b) Read the beginnings of the sentences. Then tick ✓ the correct endings.

1. *West Side Story* was originally …
   - A ☐ a film.
   - B ☐ a musical.
   - C ☐ a TV series.
2. The musical won …
   - A ☐ two Tonys.
   - B ☐ four Tonys.
   - C ☐ ten Tonys.
3. The film cost …
   - A ☐ \$4 million.
   - B ☐ \$6 million.
   - C ☐ \$44 million.
4. The film won …
   - A ☐ two Oscars.
   - B ☐ six Oscars.
   - C ☐ ten Oscars.
5. The first Drama Club performance will be …
   - A ☐ in January.
   - B ☐ in the week before Christmas.
   - C ☐ in two weeks.
6. The tickets for the Drama Club's production of *West Side Story* cost …
   - A ☐ £8.
   - B ☐ £10.
   - C ☐ £18.

c) **Listen again and match the sentence parts.**

A	Teresa's task was to
B	The Broadway musical
C	*West Side Story* is difficult because the actors
D	The original title
E	The conflict in *West Side Story*
F	Leonard Bernstein and Stephen Sondheim
G	Bernstein and Sondheim didn't like the film because it
H	The Community Centre wants to

1	was first performed in 1957.
2	watch the film at 8 pm on Friday.
3	was realistic in the 1950s.
4	have to dance, sing and act at the same time.
5	changed some of the music.
6	build a new playground.
7	prepare a presentation on famous love stories.
8	wrote the music and the lyrics.
9	was *East Side Story*.

A	
B	
C	
D	
E	
F	
G	
H	

d) **Answer the questions in complete sentences.**

1. When did work on *West Side Story* first begin?

____

2. What are the Tony Awards?

____

3. What were two of the Oscars that the film won?

____

4. How many songs are there in *West Side Story*?

____

5. How many performances will the Community Drama Club give?

____

____

6. What is Teresa's opinion of *West Side Story*?

____

____

READING

Tipp

Schritt 1 – **Vor dem Lesen:** Sieh dir die **Überschrift** an und überlege, worum es gehen könnte. Lies die Aufgabe(n) und überlege, was gesucht ist.

Schritt 2 – **Beim Lesen: Unterstreiche** die Informationen, die für die Aufgabe(n) gesucht werden.

Four true love stories

Read about four love stories from real life.

A **Juan and Evita Perón** **When:** 1940s **Where:** Argentina

What was so special about their love: Juan and Evita were a great couple who changed their country. After growing up very poor, Evita met Juan and the two fell in love. When Juan was President of Argentina, they worked together and became one of the most famous political[1] couples[2] of all time. At the young age of 33, Evita died of cancer. Their story later became a Hollywood film.

B **Richard Burton and Elizabeth Taylor** **When:** 1960s **Where:** USA

What was so special about their love: Richard Burton and Elizabeth Taylor were famous actors who worked together in many Hollywood films. They met when they made the film *Cleopatra* about the real story of Mark Antony and Cleopatra. Elizabeth Taylor played the Egyptian queen and Richard Burton played Mark Antony. When they met, they were both married to other people. They left their partners and married, but after ten years they broke up … only to marry again 16 months later! Their second break-up followed after only nine months.

C **Edward VIII and Wallis Simpson** **When:** 1930s **Where:** United Kingdom

What was so special about their love: Edward made big news – and big changes to the British monarchy[3] – when he fell in love with a married American woman, Wallis Simpson. Wallis left her husband[4] in 1934 and began a wild romance with Edward. He became king in 1936, but he wasn't allowed to marry Wallis, so he gave up his title after less than a year to be with the woman he loved.

D **Prince Rainier and Grace Kelly** **When:** 1950s **Where:** Monaco

What was so special about their love: A film star at the age of 23, American Grace Kelly gave up acting at the age of 26 to marry Prince Rainier III of Monaco and become a real-life princess. In 1982, when she was 52, Princess Grace died of injuries she received in a car accident. Prince Rainier never married again, and he died in 2005.

1 *political* [pəˈlɪtɪkəl]: politisch
2 *couple* [ˈkʌpl]: Paar
3 *monarchy* [ˈmɒnəki]: Monarchie
4 *husband* [ˈhʌzbənd]: Ehemann

a) **Match each heading to the correct text. There is one more heading than you need. Write the letters A – D in the boxes.**

☐ A Hollywood romance ☐ A king no more ☐ A real-life princess
☐ Love at first sight ☐ No happy ending

b) **Read the statements below and tick ✓ the correct boxes. There can be more than one correct answer.**

	Juan Perón/ Evita Perón	Richard Burton/ Elizabeth Taylor	Edward VIII/ Wallis Simpson	Prince Rainier/ Grace Kelly
1. They married each other twice.	☐	☐	☐	☐
2. He and/or she ended another relationship to be together with the person he or she loved.	☐	☐	☐	☐
3. He and/or she had problems with others because of his or her relationship.	☐	☐	☐	☐
4. He and/or she gave up his or her old life to be together with the person he or she loved.	☐	☐	☐	☐
5. Their love changed a country in some way.	☐	☐	☐	☐
6. Their love story became a Hollywood film.	☐	☐	☐	☐

c) **Correct the sentences.**

1. Evita's parents were very rich.

____

2. Richard Burton and Elizabeth Taylor acted together in one Hollywood film.

____

3. Wallis Simpson was British.

____

4. Prince Rainier and Princess Grace died in 2005.

____

d) Answer the questions in complete sentences.

1. Why did the story of Juan and Evita Perón end tragically?

2. How did Richard Burton and Elizabeth Taylor meet?

3. How long were Richard Burton and Elizabeth Taylor married before they broke up for the first time?

4. Why was Edward VIII only king for about a year?

5. What did Grace Kelly do before she married Prince Rainier?

6. How did the story of Prince Rainier and Princess Grace end?

WRITING

Tipp

Schritt 1 – **Vor dem Schreiben:** Prüfe, ob der Text eine bestimmte Form haben muss (z. B. E-Mail). Lege den Inhalt und die Reihenfolge fest.
Schritt 2 – **Schreibe** deinen Text.
Schritt 3 – **Überarbeite** deinen Text: Kontrolliere zuerst, ob alle Inhalte vorkommen. Prüfe dann, ob es Grammatik- oder Rechtschreibfehler gibt. Verbessere sie.

The perfect friend

☆ **An online teenage magazine has asked readers from all over the world to describe a "perfect friend". What is a perfect friend for you? Collect ideas first. You can use the ideas and phrases in the boxes or your own. Write about 80 words.**

What he/she is like	Things you do together	Things you expect from your friend
funny • interesting • clever • cool • popular • nice • good at school • likes to do sport • …	listen to music • go shopping • do sport • chat • have fun • watch films • go to parties • do homework • meet friends • …	be there for me • listen • keep our secrets • like the things I like • …

I think a perfect friend is someone who …
He/She should be …
When we spend time together, …
A perfect friend needs to …

Start like this: I think a perfect friend is someone who …

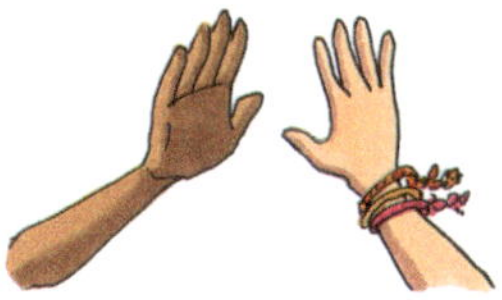

◯ *Romeo and Juliet* – like or dislike?

You have been talking about the play *Romeo and Juliet* in class. Write a review. Write about 100 words. Think about the following questions and give reasons for your opinions.

- What is the play about?
- What did you like about it? What didn't you like about it?
- How many stars do you give the play?

The words and phrases in the box will help you.

> I (don't) like the fact that … • I (don't) think that … • In my opinion, …
> The play is very / too dramatic / tragic / unrealistic / sad / exciting / romantic / …
> I give the play … stars because …

☆☆☆☆☆

Start like this: "Romeo and Juliet" is a famous play by William Shakespeare about …

Your Romeo and Juliet

In *Romeo and Juliet*, the young lovers have a lot of problems.

Romeo has had to leave Verona after a tragic fight, and Juliet's parents want her to marry Count Paris.
Juliet has taken a drug that makes her seem dead. Friar Laurence has explained this in a letter to Romeo, but Romeo has not received the letter. He comes back to Verona and finds Juliet.

Continue the story in dialogue form and write your own ending. Think about the following questions:

- Which changes do you want to make to the story?
- Do you want an open ending? A happy ending? Should Romeo and Juliet live or die?

Write about 120 words.The ideas in the box will help you.

decide to stop fighting • explain what happened • go away again • other characters arrive • talk to parents • wake up • ...

Start like this:

Romeo: Juliet! Juliet? Oh no! Is she dead? ...

MEDIATION

Tipp

Gib in deinen eigenen Worten die **wichtigen Informationen** in der jeweils **anderen Sprache** wieder. Du musst **nicht Wort für Wort** übersetzen! Passe dabei deine Ausdrucksweise der Situation und den Sprecherinnen und Sprechern an.

○ At the theatre

☆ ☾ ☼ You and your family are spending a weekend in London. You have just talked about *Romeo and Juliet* in class and would like to see the play in the theatre. Read the theatre's website and answer your parents' questions.

Dates	Saturday 20 April – Sunday 7 July
Tickets	Yard (standing) £4 Gallery (seated) £20 – £45 Under 18s: £4 off all seats in the theatre
Running time	2 hours and 45 minutes, including a break (20 minutes)

"O Romeo, Romeo, wherefore art thou Romeo?"
In Verona, two rich families hate each other. Their children choose love.

Production
A modern version of Shakespeare's famous love story with a mix of musical styles from classical music to modern pop. Please note that the production uses lighting effects and guns[1].

Audience reactions

Frances Gilbert • 7 days ago
It was fantastic! The actors were great and really brought the play to life. The music was even better than I had hoped – I loved every moment of this play!

Edward Thompson • 9 days ago
When you buy tickets to a Shakespeare play, you hope to see great actors in perfect costumes. That is not what you get here. I have never seen Shakespeare done so terribly in my life! I hated it! The modern version ruined the atmosphere completely. I wish I could get my money back for wasting three hours of my life sitting through this!

Kyle Ringrose • 22 days ago
I saw this incredible production twice when I was in London. It was everything you could want from *Romeo and Juliet*! Great costumes, fantastic actors – and the death scene really made me cry. I would see it another 20 times if I could! Go and see it!

Creatives
Writer
William Shakespeare

Director
Daniel Kausitz

Original music
Ben de Vries

Cast
Friar Laurence
Luke Sumpter

Juliet
Jane Johnson

Mercutio
Henry Tyrell

Romeo
Nathaniel Williams

Tybalt
Gregory Miller

1 *gun* [gʌn]: Schusswaffe

☆ ☾ ☼

Mother: Gut, vielleicht können wir uns das Stück ja ansehen. Was kosten denn die Tickets?

You: Stehplätze ______________________________

Sitzplätze ______________________________

Father: Gibt es auch ermäßigte Karten für dich und deinen kleinen Bruder?

You: Ja, die Sitzplätze ______________________________

____

Mother: Und wie lang ist das Stück?

You: Das Stück dauert ______________________________

Es gibt aber auch ______________________________

☾ ☼

Father: Steht da auch, worum es geht?

You: In dem Stück geht es um ______________________________

____

____

____

Mother: Was sollte man denn über die Produktion wissen? Ist sie zum Beispiel eher modern oder eher klassisch?

You: Sie ist eher ______________. Die Musik ______________

____

Außerdem ______________________________

____

Father: Und wer sind die Hauptdarsteller, also Romeo und Julia?

You: Der Darsteller des Romeo heißt ______________________________

____

____

____

☼

Mother: Was sagen denn die Leute, die das Stück schon gesehen haben?

You: Es gibt mehrere Meinungen zu dem Stück. Frances Gilbert zum Beispiel schreibt, dass

____

Kyle Ringrose meint, ______________________________

Allerdings ist Edward Thompson der Meinung, dass ______________________________

Ich denke, wir müssen einfach selbst herausfinden, ob es uns gefällt.

WORDS AND GRAMMAR

Definitions

Match the words to the definitions.

A	part of a tree
B	another word for "if"
C	a person who hates you
D	someone who tells actors what to do
E	to make somebody stop sleeping
F	a kind of relationship

1	friendship
2	to wake somebody up
3	director
4	fight
5	branch
6	whether
7	enemy

A	
B	
C	
D	
E	
F	

Verbs, verbs, verbs

Complete the crossword puzzle and find the solution word.

1. to become bigger or taller
2. to agree that something is true even though you don't want to
3. to look at somebody for a long time
4. to go with or in front of someone to show them the way
5. to walk past somebody or something
6. to see or hear something
7. to become impossible[1] to see

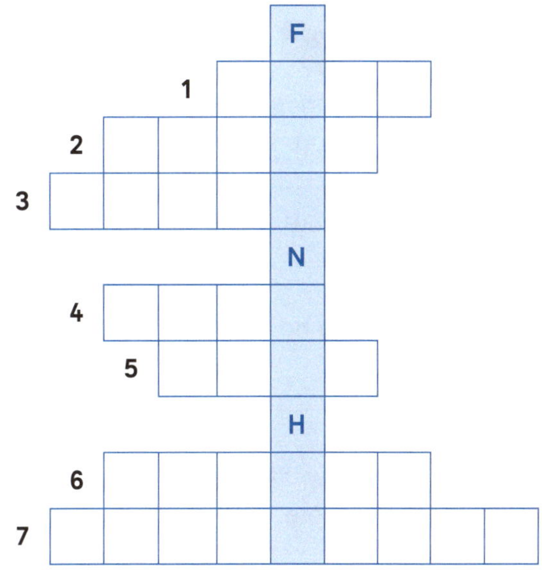

Solution word:

F				N			H		

1 *impossible* [ɪmˈpɒsəbl]: unmöglich

Opposites

Write down the opposites.

1. every one ⟷ ______________________
2. clever ⟷ ______________________
3. life ⟷ ______________________
4. follow ⟷ ______________________
5. hate ⟷ ______________________
6. safe ⟷ ______________________
7. gain ⟷ ______________________
8. friend ⟷ ______________________

Phrases

Match the parts to complete the phrases.

A	wake
B	stare
C	seem
D	watch
E	have
F	get to

1	asleep
2	a big fight
3	at somebody
4	a quote from a book
5	a play in the theatre
6	somebody up
7	know somebody

A	
B	
C	
D	
E	
F	

More words

Complete the sentences with the words from the box. Be careful to use the correct forms. There is one more word than you need.

fight • grow • conversation • date • admit • lead • disappear

1. David likes Myra, so he asked her out on a ______________________.
2. My grandparents ______________________ vegetables in their garden – they're delicious!
3. Megan's favourite sweater has ______________________. She can't find it anywhere.

4. Many people think that Hollywood stars ______________________ very interesting lives.
5. Some people use chat-up lines to start a ______________________ with someone they like.
6. When you've had a ______________________ with a friend, it's often best to say sorry.

Some chat-up lines

Complete these chat-up lines. Use the words from the box or your own ideas.

know • lose • dinosaurs • disappear • come to earth • socks

1. Kiss me if I'm wrong but ____________________

____

2. Are you a magician? Because ____________________

____

3. I didn't know that angels ____________________

4. ____________________ we would make a great pair.

5. ____________________? You look exactly like my next girlfriend.

Send me an email

In each of the following sentences there is a verb with two objects. Use different colours to underline the indirect object (usually a person) and the direct object (usually a thing). Then complete the sentences, putting the two objects in the correct order.

1. her friends • emails

Mary often sends ____________________.

2. some chocolate • my grandfather

I usually take ____________________ when I visit him.

3. her boyfriend • a beautiful card

Lisa made ____________________ for Valentine's Day.

4. her brother • a cool CD

Ayla gave ____________________ for his birthday.

5. his friends • a picture of his girlfriend

Timothy showed ____________________ on his mobile.

6. lots of questions • his classmates

After the holidays Rohit asked ____________________.

7. her family and friends • little presents

Ciara buys ____________________ whenever she's on holiday.

Unscramble the following sentences and write them down. Each of your sentences will have a verb with two objects, for example: give + me + your answer. Find the verb and the two objects and underline them in the same colours as here.

1. his friends • Liam • more than 100 messages • sends • every day

Liam ______________________________

2. Robbie • his girlfriend • a ring • promised

Robbie ______________________________

3. always • money • Aisha • her best friend • gives

Aisha ______________________________

4. her friend • Ria • her English book • gave

Ria ______________________________

5. gives • Jason • his English homework • his friend Sarah • always

Jason ______________________________

6. something sweet from her parents' shop • Naomi • her friends • takes • always

Naomi ______________________________

7. every time she visits him • Lynn • her grandfather • gives • a little present

Lynn ______________________________

Give the information in one sentence with two objects, for example: give + me + your answer. Find the verb and the two objects and underline them in the same colours as in the example.

Example: Valeria brought flowers to say sorry. She brought them to her boyfriend.

Valeria brought her boyfriend flowers to say sorry.

1. Eliza writes a lot of letters. She writes them to her friends.

2. Greg told a funny story. He told it to Bert.

3. Peter made a mixed CD for Valentine's Day. He made it for his girlfriend.

4. Jamie bought a big birthday present. He bought it for Oliver.

5. Raj showed photos of his trip to India. He showed them to his friends.

6. His parents asked Neil. They asked a lot of questions about his new girlfriend.

7. Layla's grandmother sent a present. She sent it to Layla.

In Verona

Complete the sentences with the adverbs from the box. There is one more adverb than you need.

proudly • dangerously • quietly • well • sadly • shyly

1. The Capulets and the Montagues talk ____________________ about themselves.
2. At first, Romeo and Juliet only look at each other ____________________ .
3. Romeo and Juliet speak ____________________ because they don't want to be heard.
4. When her father tells Juliet that she must marry Count Paris, she looks at him __________.
5. When Juliet wakes up, she knows that her plan has not gone ____________________ .

Use the adverb forms of the adjectives in brackets () to complete the sentences.

1. The Capulets and the Montagues fight each other openly ____________________ (open).
2. When Juliet arrives at the party, she smiles ____________________ (happy).
3. When Romeo sees Juliet, he falls ____________________ (mad) in love with her.
4. Tybalt hurts Mercutio so ____________________ (severe) that Mercutio dies.
5. Juliet goes to Friar Laurence ____________________ (secret) and talks to him.
6. When Juliet wakes up, she opens her eyes ____________________ (slow).

Complete the sentences with the adverb forms of the adjectives in the box. There are two more adjectives than you need.

incredible • important • angry • sweet • bad • easy • happy • fast

1. Benvolio ____________________ convinces[1] Romeo to go to the ball.
2. When Romeo sees Juliet, he thinks she is ____________________ beautiful.
3. Tybalt and Romeo fight ____________________.
4. Romeo must leave Verona ____________________.
5. Friar Laurence thinks the love story of Romeo and Juliet will end ____________________ .
6. However, the story ends ____________________ for the young lovers.

1 *to convince sb* [kən'vɪns]: jdn. überzeugen

More than ever

Circle the correct comparative forms of the adverbs.

1. I have never seen Lisa look at anyone **colder / more coldly** than at her ex-boyfriend.
2. When Akello is with his new best friend, he talks **more loudly / most loudly** than ever.
3. Matilda has never cried **most terribly / more terribly** than when Mark left her.
4. When Julia is with Ruben, she speaks **more nervously / most nervously** than usual.
5. Kojo tried **hardly / harder** than ever before to be nice to his new girlfriend's parents.
6. The next time Leroy helps him, Paolo should thank him **more grateful / more gratefully**.

Use the adverbs in the box to complete the sentences. There is one more adverb than you need. Use each adverb only once.

better • more healthily • more sadly • more shyly • more happily • more carefully • more easily

1. Breaking up with Lee was hard for Faye, but she can talk about it ________________ now.
2. Ebo's new girlfriend is good for him. He even plays football ________________ than before.
3. Callum smiles at his girlfriend ________________________________ than ever before.
4. Leila got a few bad marks in maths, so she does her homework ________________ now.
5. Since Mika met Joy, he has been going to the gym and eating much ________________.
6. Ahmet had never spoken ____________________ than when he asked Eliza out on a date.

Use the adverbs in the box to complete the sentences. There are three more adverbs than you need. Use each adverb only once.

more slowly • more importantly • more bitterly • more openly • more angrily • faster • more beautifully • harder • more severely

1. I have never seen Isla cry ________________________ than when she broke up with Carl.
2. Jay has a new coach now, and he is running ____________________________ than ever.
3. Mateo shouted ______________________ than ever when he saw Zoe with someone else.
4. Fleur can talk to Ben ______________________ than to anyone else. He understands her.
5. Victoria's boyfriend is really good at school, so she is working much ______________ now.
6. Uncle Bert should really drive ______________________. It's dangerous to drive that fast.

A terrible date

Ally is on a terrible date with Jake. Whenever she can, she sends her best friend text messages about it. What does Jake say? Match the reported speech with the right sentences. Write the numbers 1 – 6 in the boxes. There are more sentences than you need.

1. Jake says he is sorry that he nearly forgot our date!
2. Jake knows that I don't like Mexican food, but he says I'm going to like it.
3. Jake asks whether I like action films, but I don't.
4. Jake says we should watch the new Bruce Willis film together.
5. Jake asks if I would like to try his food even though he knows I'm a vegetarian.
6. Jake says I shouldn't have any dessert. I'm leaving.

- ☐ Do you like action films?
- ☐ We should watch the new Bruce Willis film together.
- ☐ Would you like to try my food?
- ☐ Sorry, you nearly forgot our date!
- ☐ You shouldn't have any dessert.
- ☐ Sorry, I nearly forgot our date!
- ☐ Don't worry; you're going to like it.
- ☐ You don't like Mexican food?
- ☐ Are you a vegetarian?

Fernanda is on a terrible date with Zevi. Whenever she can, she sends her best friend text messages about it. What does she write? Complete the sentences in reported speech.

1. Zevi: "Do you like sushi?"

Zevi asks ______________________________

2. Zevi: "We're going to have some anyway."

He says that we ______________________________

3. Zevi: "Do you always wear sports clothes when you are on a date?"

Zevi asks whether ______________________________

4. Zevi: "When I first met you, I didn't like you at all."

Zevi says when he first ______________________

____

5. Zevi: "If you don't want your sushi, I'll eat it."

He says if I ______________________

____

6. Zevi: "This date was a very good idea."

Zevi thinks ______________________

Leif is on a terrible date with Jessalyn. Whenever he can, he sends his best friend text messages about it. What does he write? Rewrite the sentences in reported speech.

1. Jessalyn: "I wanted to say no at first."

Jessalyn says that she ______________________

2. Jessalyn: "Are you paying for this dinner?"

She wants to know ______________________

3. Jessalyn: "I'm the girl so I'm going to pick the film."

____

____

4. Jessalyn: "You have gained weight since I last saw you."

____

____

5. Jessalyn: "Do you still work at that stupid comic book store?"

____

____

6. Jessalyn: "The food here is terrible. Why didn't you choose a nice restaurant?"

____

____

What do they ask?

What do the people want to know? Complete the sentences.

1. *Juliet to herself:* "Why does Romeo have to be a Montague?"

2. *Capulet to Juliet:* "Why don't you want to marry Count Paris?"

3. *Romeo to Juliet:* "Will you marry me?"

4. *Friar Laurence to Juliet:* "How can I help you?"

5. *Romeo to himself:* "Is there a way to stop the fighting?"

6. *Montague to Capulet:* "How can we become friends?"

1. Juliet asks herself why Romeo ______________________ a Montague.
2. Capulet asks Juliet why she ______________________ Count Paris.
3. Romeo asks Juliet whether she ______________________ him.
4. Friar Laurence asks Juliet how ______________________ her.
5. Romeo wonders if ______________________ a way to stop the fighting.
6. Montague asks Capulet how ______________________ become friends.

What do the people want to know? Complete the sentences.

1. *Juliet to herself:* "When will Romeo be back?"

Juliet asks herself when ______________________

2. *Capulet to Juliet:* "What are you going to wear to the party tonight?"

Capulet asks Juliet what ______________________

3. *Romeo to Juliet:* "Do you love me?"

Romeo asks Juliet if ______________________

4. *Friar Laurence to Juliet:* "Are you ready to take the drug?"

Friar Laurence asks Juliet whether ______________________________

5. *Romeo to himself:* "Why do our families have to be enemies?"

Romeo wonders why ______________________________

6. *Capulet to Montague:* "Did you know about Romeo and Juliet?"

Capulet asks Montague if ______________________________

Rewrite what these people say in reported speech.

1. *Juliet to herself:* "Will my father make me marry Count Paris?"

Juliet asks herself ______________________________

____

____

2. *Capulet to Juliet:* "Who were you just talking to?"

____

____

3. *Romeo to Juliet:* "Can you forget my name?"

____

____

4. *Friar Laurence to Juliet:* "Do you want to leave Verona with Romeo?"

____

____

5. *Romeo to himself (after killing Juliet's cousin):* "Will Juliet still love me?"

____

____

6. *Capulet to Montague:* "How can we ever forgive[1] ourselves?"

____

____

1 *to forgive* [fəˈgɪv]: verzeihen, vergeben

SPEAKING

○ Let's talk about *Romeo and Juliet*

Tipp

Schritt 1 – Überlege, was du sagen möchtest und **welche Worte** du dafür benötigst.
Schritt 2 – Sprich in **ganzen Sätzen**. Umschreibe Worte, die dir nicht einfallen, **auf Englisch**.

☆ **Talk about the play *Romeo and Juliet*. Look at the pictures and say what the play is about. The phrases from the boxes will help you.**

The play is about ... • In the famous play *Romeo and Juliet*, ...
two lovers • a young couple • enemies • ...
fall in love • marry secretly • fight • kill • ...
look dead • be asleep • kill himself/herself • ...

Romeo • Juliet
Montague • Capulet
Friar Laurence

☾ **Have you ever read or seen a love story as tragic as that of Romeo and Juliet? Talk about it. Think about the following questions:**

- **What is the book/film about?**
- **What makes the story sad/tragic?**
- **How does the story end?**
- **Did you like it? Why/Why not?**

The words and phrases in the box will help you.

The film/book is called ... • It is about ... • The story is sad/tragic because ... •
two lovers • a young couple • enemies • fall in love • marry • get very ill •
die • kill • At the end, ... • I liked/didn't like the film/book because ...

☼ **Talk about the play *Romeo and Juliet*. Think about the following questions:**

- **Who wrote the play?**
- **What is the play about?**
- **Did you like it? Why/Why not?**

LISTENING

Tipp

Schritt 1 – **Vor dem ersten Hören:** Lies die Aufgabe(n).
Schritt 2 – **Beim ersten Hören:** Bearbeite die Aufgabe(n).
Schritt 3 – **Beim zweiten Hören:** Vervollständige und verbessere deine Antworten.

Stacey's work experience

a) Listen to Stacey Thomas talking to a school reporter. Tick ✓ the three things she is talking about.

☐ her future job
☐ her last job
☐ her new job in a hair salon
☐ her parents' jobs
☐ her tasks during her work experience
☐ her work experience in a hair salon

b) Read the sentence beginnings and endings. Listen again and tick ✓ the correct endings.

1. Stacey is in …
   A ☐ year seven.
   B ☐ year eight.
   C ☐ year nine.
2. Fair Hair is …
   A ☐ close to Stacey's house.
   B ☐ in the city centre.
   C ☐ near Stacey's school.
3. During her first week Stacey had to …
   A ☐ give customers magazines.
   B ☐ clean the coffee maker.
   C ☐ buy shampoo for the customers.
4. In the second week, Stacey helped to …
   A ☐ colour hair.
   B ☐ pick the colour out of people's clothes.
   C ☐ put shampoo in people's hair.
5. Stacey liked her work experience and …
   A ☐ she learned a lot about the job.
   B ☐ she earned a lot of money.
   C ☐ she was very careful.
6. Stacey didn't like …
   A ☐ most of the customers.
   B ☐ standing all day.
   C ☐ the working hours.

c) Listen again and tick ✓ right or wrong.

	right	wrong
1. Stacey's work experience lasted two weeks.	☐	☐
2. She liked the hairdressers who worked at the salon.	☐	☐
3. During her first week, Stacey had to clean the toilets.	☐	☐
4. Stacey found colouring hair difficult because the colour mustn't get on people's skin or clothes.	☐	☐
5. Before you can cut anyone's hair, you have to watch an experienced hairdresser two or three times.	☐	☐
6. Stacey had one long break and two short breaks every day.	☐	☐
7. Stacey would like to be a famous hairdresser one day.	☐	☐

d) Correct the wrong sentences from c).

____

____

____

____

____

e) Answer the questions in complete sentences.

1. How many people work at Fair Hair?

____

2. What do you have to be careful about when washing a customer's hair?

____

____

3. Why were some of the customers a little mean towards Stacey?

____

____

4. When did Stacey start and finish work every day?

____

____

____

READING

Tipp

Schritt 1 – **Vor dem Lesen:** Sieh dir die **Überschrift** an und überlege, worum es gehen könnte. Lies die Aufgabe(n) und überlege, was gesucht ist.
Schritt 2 – **Beim Lesen: Unterstreiche** die Informationen, die für die Aufgabe(n) gesucht werden.

Success can start in a garage

Read the text about the computer industry in the USA.

A After 1945, many universities[1] in the USA had a problem. The Second World War[2] was over, a great number of young men were coming back home – and many of them wanted to study. The universities needed money to make that happen, including Stanford University near San Francisco, California, one of the best universities in the USA. In 1951, Professor Frederick Terman had an idea: He created Stanford Industrial Park and let only high-tech companies[3] rent[4] the land there.

B In the 1970s, traditional American industries began to disappear. Many people in the steel[5] industry and in the car and shoe factories lost their jobs. Some companies moved[6] to other countries; others closed because it was cheaper to buy products from abroad. In the 1980s, new industries were needed. There were many new inventions in the world of computers, and many new high-tech companies were founded[7]. Lots of young inventors wanted to be part of that – and because most of them didn't have a lot of money at first, they worked at home, in their garages.

C When the computer industry started to grow in the late 1980s, small businesses moved out of their garages and became large companies. Many of them moved to the area around San José, California, where everything had started with the foundation of Stanford Industrial Park in the 1950s. Now called Stanford Research Park, it is now home to more than 150 companies that employ about 23,000 people. The whole San José area has been called Silicon Valley[8] since the early 1970s because of the silicon that is needed to make computer chips.

D Make no mistake – Silicon Valley is about much more than producing computer chips today. When the Internet became available to a larger number of people in the mid-1990s, many new companies tried their luck in Silicon Valley. The area has become the centre of high-tech, software and Internet companies, and is home to many of the biggest and most successful businesses in the world. Today, about 250,000 people live and work in the area. If you can afford it, Silicon Valley is one of the best places in the USA to live – but it is also one of the most expensive. The area also has amazing weather: 300 days of sunshine every year may explain why people seem to be so happy there.

1 *university* [ˌjuːnɪˈvɜːsəti]: Universität
2 *the Second World War* [wɔː]: der Zweite Weltkrieg
3 *company* [ˈkʌmpəni]: Firma, Unternehmen
4 *rent* [rent]: mieten
5 *steel* [stiːl]: Stahl
6 *move* [muːv]: umziehen
7 *found* [faʊnd]: gründen
8 *valley* [ˈvæli]: Tal

a) Match each heading to the correct part of the text. There are more headings than you need.

A changing world • A very big idea • From the garage to Silicon Valley • How to be successful in Silicon Valley • Software companies leave the USA • The centre of the Internet

A ______

B ______

C ______

D ______

b) Read the sentences and tick ✓ right or wrong.

	right	wrong
1. In the 1940s, Stanford University did not have enough students.	☐	☐
2. Frederick Terman wanted Stanford Industrial Park to make money.	☐	☐
3. A lot of workers in traditional industries lost their jobs in the 1970s.	☐	☐
4. Garages were a cheap workplace for young inventors.	☐	☐
5. About 23,000 people work in Stanford Research Park today.	☐	☐
6. The area around San José has always been known as Silicon Valley.	☐	☐
7. Silicon Valley is important today because many computer chips are made there.	☐	☐
8. The weather is extremely good in Silicon Valley.	☐	☐

c) Correct the wrong sentences from b).

______

______

______

______

______

______

______

______

______

d) Answer the questions in complete sentences.

1. What problem did American universities face after the Second World War?

2. Who can rent land in Stanford Industrial Park?

3. How did the computer industry develop in the 1980s?

4. What new development happened in Silicon Valley in the 1990s?

5. What makes Silicon Valley a popular place to live today? What might make living there difficult?

WRITING

Tipp

Schritt 1 – **Vor dem Schreiben:** Prüfe, ob der Text eine bestimmte Form haben muss (z. B. E-Mail). Lege den Inhalt und die Reihenfolge fest.
Schritt 2 – **Schreibe** deinen Text.
Schritt 3 – **Überarbeite** deinen Text: Kontrolliere zuerst, ob alle Inhalte vorkommen. Prüfe dann, ob es Grammatik- oder Rechtschreibfehler gibt. Verbessere sie.

My dream job

What is your dream job? Think about the following questions:

- What job would you like to do?
- What tasks will you have to do?
- What hard and soft skills will you need?
- Why do you think you would enjoy the job?

Write about 80 words. The words and phrases in the boxes will help you.

I would like/love to work as a(n) … I think a job as a(n) … would be …	doctor's assistant • firefighter • gardener • hairdresser • software developer • teacher • …
As a(n) …, you have to … A(n) … usually does/works/has to … A(n) … needs to know a lot about …	help people who are ill • deal with dangerous situations • read a lot • know a lot about plants • …
You need to have … You should be able to …	communication/customer service/ organizational skills • be on time • be nice • work in a team • …
I think that being a … is great because … I would enjoy the job because …	help other people • meet interesting people • spend time outdoors • work on interesting projects • exciting • important • well-paid • …

Start like this: I would like to work as a(n) …

Hard skills and soft skills

A local baker is looking for someone to help out for a few hours every Sunday. You have been invited for a job interview. To prepare for the interview, write a short text about why you are the right person for the job. Think about the following questions:

- What tasks will you have to do?
- What hard and soft skills will you need?
- Why would you be good at the job?

Write about 100 words. The words and phrases in the box will help you.

answer questions • be nice • have work experience • sell bread/cake • speak different languages • start work early • talk to customers • work in a team • …

Start like this: I think that I am the right person for the job because …

The job interview

A local petrol station is looking for someone to help out for three hours every Saturday. You have been invited for a job interview. Write a dialogue between yourself and the staff manager, Mrs Muir. Think about:

- what questions Mrs Muir will probably ask
- what hard and soft skills you will need
- why you would be good at/enjoy the job.

Remember to be polite[1]. Write about 120 words. The ideas in the box will help you.

available • vexperience • favourite subjects • maths • languages • teamwork • customer service • …

1 *polite* [pəˈlaɪt]: höflich

Start like this:

Mrs Muir: Welcome, … . Thank you for coming here today.

You:

MEDIATION

Tipp

Gib in deinen eigenen Worten die **wichtigen Informationen** in der jeweils **anderen Sprache** wieder. Du musst **nicht Wort für Wort** übersetzen! Passe dabei deine Ausdrucksweise der Situation und den Sprecherinnen und Sprechern an.

○ 112 days in outer space

Your English friend has to prepare a presentation on unusual jobs. You have found this interview with German astronaut Dr Kristina Gebauer online and want to tell your friend about it. Read the interview and answer your friend's questions.

„Ich habe mich gefühlt wie R2D2."

Nach 112 Tagen hat Kristina Gebauer nun wieder festen Boden unter den Füßen. Beinahe vier Monate lang war die Wissenschaftlerin gemeinsam mit fünf anderen Astronauten aus verschiedenen Ländern an Bord der Internationalen Raumstation ISS und arbeitete an etwa 80 Experimenten, bevor sie Ende August auf die Erde zurückkehrte. Dies ist ihr erstes Interview.

Frau Gebauer, wie sind Sie eigentlich Astronautin geworden?

Kristina Gebauer: Ich wollte eigentlich schon immer die Erde aus dem Weltraum sehen, aber man braucht schon viel Glück. Es gibt sehr viele, die sich bewerben – und auf der ISS ist ja nicht viel Platz, da sind immer nur sechs Personen. Vor ziemlich genau sechs Jahren suchte die ESA, die European Space Agency, online neue Astronautinnen und Astronauten. Das musste ich einfach versuchen. Als ich ausgewählt wurde, war das ein tolles Gefühl. Ich hatte noch nicht einmal meiner Familie von meiner Bewerbung erzählt, weil ich dachte, es würde ohnehin nicht klappen.

Sie sind Physikerin[1] – wie wichtig war das für Ihre Bewerbung?

Kristina Gebauer: Es gibt alle möglichen Berufe unter Astronauten: Piloten, Ingenieure, Wissenschaftler oder auch Ärzte. Wichtig ist, dass man sich mit Wissenschaft auskennt, dass man schnell und klug mit Problemen umgehen kann und mit neuen Situationen zurechtkommt. Man muss auch gut mit Stress umgehen können – auf der ISS ist kein Platz, um wegzulaufen oder sich zu verstecken. Alles andere lernt man beim Astronautentraining sowieso neu.

Was haben Sie auf der ISS genau gemacht?

Kristina Gebauer: Genau wie auf der Erde muss man auch auf der ISS abwechselnd arbeiten und hat frei. Allerdings sind die Freizeitmöglichkeiten natürlich stark eingeschränkt. Während der Arbeitszeit habe ich eine ganze Reihe von Experimenten gemacht. Wissenschaftler aus ganz Europa haben diese Experimente entwickelt und wir haben sie durchgeführt. Manchmal musste man nur auf einen Knopf[2] drücken[3] und aufschreiben, was passiert, aber manche Experimente sind eben auch kompliziert. Einmal mussten wir eine komplizierte Maschine sehr schnell reparieren. Da habe ich mich ein bisschen gefühlt wie R2D2.

Eine letzte Frage: Wird eigentlich auf der ISS immer Englisch gesprochen?

Kristina Gebauer: Von allem ein bisschen. Im amerikanischen Teil der ISS sprechen wir Englisch, aber man kann ja auch voneinander lernen. Man versucht, immer ein bisschen die Sprache der anderen zu sprechen. Das ergibt einen lustigen Mix – dabei hatten wir viel Spaß!

1 Physiker/in: *physicist* [ˈfɪzɪsɪst] 2 Knopf: *button* [ˈbʌtən] 3 drücken: *push* [pʊʃ]

☆ ☾ ☼

Friend: Dr Gebauer is back on earth now, right? How long was she in space?

You: Yes, she is ______________________________

____

____

____

____

Friend: She wasn't on the ISS alone, was she? Who else was there?

You: No, of course she wasn't! ______________________________

____

Friend: What made her want to become an astronaut?

You: Dr Gebauer says that ______________________________

____

____

Friend: How did she become an astronaut? Was it difficult to become one?

You: She says that ESA ______________________________

____

____

☾ ☼

Friend: How did she feel when she was chosen? Was she surprised?

You: She was very ______________________________

____

____

____

Friend: What kind of profession do you need to have if you want to be an astronaut?

You: Well, she says that ______________________________

____

____

Friend: What skills does an astronaut need?

You: She says that you need to ________________

____

____

____

____

____

____

☼

Friend: What does she say about her work on the ISS?

You: Her job was to do ____

____

____

____

____

____

____

____

____

Friend: How did she communicate with the other astronauts?

You: When she was in the American part of the ISS, ________________

____

____

____

____

____

WORDS AND GRAMMAR

Words, words, words

Where do these people work? Find the right nouns.

1. waiter/waitress – ____________________
2. doctor's assistant – ____________________
3. flight attendant – ____________________
4. secretary – ____________________
5. teacher – ____________________
6. farmer – ____________________
7. gardener – ____________________
8. lifeguard – ____________________

Complete the text with the words from the box. Be careful to use the correct form. There is one more word than you need.

fail • develop • training • work placement • study • heating system • patient • rescue • try

There are many different jobs. A software developer has to ____________________ new computer programmes. A plumber has to install ____________________. As a lifeguard, you must keep fit so you're able to ____________________ people. If you're not sure what kind of job is right for you, you should do one or more ____________________ to find out what you enjoy and what you are good at. You should ____________________ different jobs before you decide. Perhaps you would like to do ____________________ as a nurse or even ____________________ to become a doctor? Take your time and be ____________________, and you will find out what kind of job would be right for you.

Fill in the missing words.

verb	noun
train	
	creation
	release
result	

verb	noun
	development
produce	
	offer
	demonstration

Phrases

Complete the phrases with the words from the box. There are more words than you need.

a seat • a result • fall • improve • an example • offer • down • apply

1. take ______________________
2. give ______________________
3. sit ______________________
5. ______________________ for a job
6. ______________________ asleep
7. ______________________ your soft skills

Skills

a) Put the skills from the box in the correct lists.

typing • politeness • ability to work in a team • speaking different languages • organizational skills • reliability • computer programming • cooking

hard skills	soft skills

b) Find two more skills for each list.

c) Which of the skills from a) and b) do you have? Write four sentences and give examples.

One of my skills is ______________________. For example, ______________________

Career advice

Tipp

Wenn du sagen willst, was unter bestimmten Bedingungen geschehen wird oder kann, verwendest du den Bedingungssatz 1:

If you **become** a flight attendant,	you **will travel** a lot.
if-Satz *(simple present)*	Hauptsatz *(will-future)*

Jeremy is not sure what he wants to do when he leaves school, so he asks for advice. Complete the sentences.

1. If you are good at maths, you ________________ (not have) any problems finding a job.
2. If you want to train as a web designer, you ________________________ (have to) apply for a job soon.
3. If you study medicine, you ________________________ (take) a lot of exams.
4. If you study abroad, you ________________________ (improve) your language skills.
5. If you want to work on your soft skills, you ________________ (find) courses online.
6. If you are late for a job interview, you ________________________ (not make) a good impression.

Jessie is not sure what she wants to do when she leaves school, so she asks for advice. Complete the sentences. Use conditional 1.

1. If you become (become) a scientist, you ________________ (do) many interesting experiments.
2. If you ________________ (go) to university[1], you ________________ (need) a lot of books.
3. If you ________________ (work) as a doctor's assistant, you ________________ (help) people who are ill.
4. If you ________________ (not decide) what you want to do soon, you ________________ (not have) a job next summer.
5. If you ________________ (not find) the right job, you ________________ (not enjoy) your work.
6. If you ________________ (write) to that company[2], I'm sure they ________________ (invite) you for a job interview.

1 *university* [ˌjuːnɪˈvɜːsəti]: Universität   2 *company* [ˈkʌmpni]: Firma, Unternehmen

What would a career advisor[1] tell a student? Write sentences. Use conditional 1.

Example: you • choose an unusual job – you • learn many new skills

If you choose an unusual job, you will learn many new skills.

1. you • work abroad for a year – you • meet many interesting people

If you work ______________________________

2. you • decide to study – you • learn some hard skills

____

3. you • train as a nurse – you • not have easy working hours

____

4. you • not try harder – you • not find a job

____

5. you • not find a work placement soon – I • help you

____

6. you • need help applying for a job – I • check your letter for you

____

1 *advisor* [ədˈvaɪzə]: Berater/in

Jobs and duties

Complete the text with the correct forms of the modal verbs from the box. Use each verb only once. There is one more verb than you need.

mustn't • not have to • be able to • shouldn't • be allowed to • should • have to

1. A doctor ______________________ be nice to his or her patients if they are scared.
2. A gardener must ______________________ tell you a lot about different plants.
3. A software developer ______________________ spend a lot of time at the office.
4. A hairdresser ______________________ work late at night.
5. A police officer ______________________ let anyone get away with stolen things.
6. A lifeguard ______________________ tell people to leave the swimming pool.

Complete the sentences with the modal verbs from the box. There is one more verb than you need. Be careful to use the correct forms of the verbs.

be allowed to • have to • shouldn't • can • needn't • be able to • not be allowed to

1. A nurse ______________________________ be afraid of seeing some bad injuries.
2. My grandfather was a firefighter. He often ______________________________ deal with dangerous situations.
3. My sister wants to work in a bank later. She ______________________________ talk about her customers' money to other people.
4. A doctor must ____________________ remember a lot of facts about the human body.
5. When my grandmother was a child, teachers ______________________ hit the pupils.
6. Our neighbour is a flight attendant. He ____________________________ tell you lots of stories about different countries.

Write sentences with the correct forms of the modal verbs from the box. There can be more than one solution and you can use the same verb more than once.

not be able to • can • not have to • shouldn't • mustn't • not be allowed to • have to

1. teacher • give the pupils homework

____

2. in 1850 • women • become doctors

____

3. musician • forget the words of a song during a concert

____

____

4. artist • have a lot of ideas

____

5. flight attendant • fly a plane

____

6. secretary • be able to swim

____

If only ...

Tipp

Wenn eine Bedingung unwahrscheinlich oder unmöglich ist, verwendest du den Bedingungssatz 2:

If my parents **had** more money,	they **would send** me to art school.
if-Satz *(simple past)*	Hauptsatz *(would/could* + Infinitiv)

Complete the sentences. Use *would* and one of the verbs from the box. There is one more verb than you need.

get • develop • play • help • make • be • spend

1. If Eliza tidied her room more often, she ______________ less time looking for things.
2. If Becca believed in herself more, her soft skills ______________ much better.
3. If Mika used his computer for school, he ______________ some useful skills.
4. If Liv concentrated more, she ______________ much better marks.
5. If Greg went to France, it ______________ him with his language skills.
6. If Miles trained a little harder, he ______________ tennis well enough to become a professional.

Complete the sentences with the correct forms of the verbs in brackets (). Use conditional 2.

1. If Jack spent (spend) less time playing hockey, he ______________ (have) more time for his homework.
2. If Hannah ______________ (apply) for a work placement at the hotel, I'm sure they ______________ (invite) her for an interview.
3. If Joshua ______________ (not be) so nervous, his job interviews ______________ (go) better.
4. If Katie ______________ (not have) such good marks, she ______________ (not be able) to train to become a software developer.
5. If Chloe ______________ (leave) the house a little earlier, she ______________ (not get) into trouble for being late every day.
6. If Matthew ______________ (develop) his communication skills, he ______________ (find) a job more easily.

Complete the sentences. Use conditional 2.

1. If Ellie had an afternoon job, she ______
2. If Callum did his homework every day, ______
3. If Lewis had more pocket money, ______
4. If Connor improved his soft skills, ______
______
5. If Grace found someone to help with her history presentation, ______
______
6. If Charlotte took part in the maths competition at school, ______
______

Work experience

Tipp

Wenn bei der indirekten Rede der Begleitsatz in der Vergangenheit steht, musst du die Zeitform anpassen *(backshift of tenses)*, z. B. *simple present → simple past*. Wenn du nicht sicher bist, kannst du im TB auf S. 191 (LiF 16) nachsehen.

Report what these pupils said about their work experience. Complete the sentences.

1. Miranda: "I'm doing my work experience as a secretary."

Miranda said that she ______ her work experience as a secretary.

2. Kalen and Keira: "We're happy to work together."

Kalen and Keira said that they ______ happy to work together.

3. Ben: "My work experience is really boring."

Ben said that his work experience ______ really boring.

4. Kimberly: "I'm learning a lot at the doctor's office."

Kimberly said that she ______ a lot at the doctor's office.

5. Abdul: "My boss is teaching me a lot about the job."

Abdul said that his boss ______ him a lot about the job.

6. Jeff: "I'll ask if I can work here in the summer."

Jeff said that he ______ if he ______ there in the summer.

Report what these pupils said about their work experience.

1. Violet: "I'm thinking of becoming a doctor's assistant."

Violet said that she ______________________________

2. Chang: "I have to be at work at 7.30 am."

Chang said that he ______________________________

3. Mila: "I don't want to work as a hairdresser anymore."

Mila said that she ______________________________

4. Linus: "Dealing with customers can be really hard sometimes."

Linus said that ______________________________

5. Alexei: "I can't wait to go back to school."

Alexei said that he ______________________________

6. Riya: "I hope I can work here again during the summer."

Riya said that she ______________________________

a) Report what these pupils said about their work experience.

1. Nigel: "I'll be sorry when my work experience is over."

Nigel said that ______________________________

2. Vasili: "I don't understand why we have to do work experience."

____

3. Daria: "I'm having a really good time!"

____

b) What else did they say? Use direct speech.

1. Victoria said that she really enjoyed feeling useful.

Victoria: "I really ______________________________

2. Katherine said that some of her tasks were a little boring.

Katherine: "______________________________

3. Ryan said he was going to apply for a job as a gardener after school.

Ryan: "______________________________

SPEAKING

The right job

Work with a partner. Talk about jobs.

Partner A

You are trying to decide what kind of job might be right for you. Talk to B and ask for advice.

Think about the following questions:
- What are you good at (school subjects, hard skills, soft skills)?
- What do you enjoy doing? What do you like about it?
- Have you already done work experience? How did you like it?
- Has B already done work experience? How did he/she like it?

Partner B

A is trying to decide what kind of job might be right for him/her. Talk to A and give advice.

Think about the following questions:
- What is A good at (school subjects, hard skills, soft skills)?
- What does A enjoy doing? What does he/she like about it?
- Has A already done work experience? How did he/she like it?
- Have you already done work experience? How did you like it?

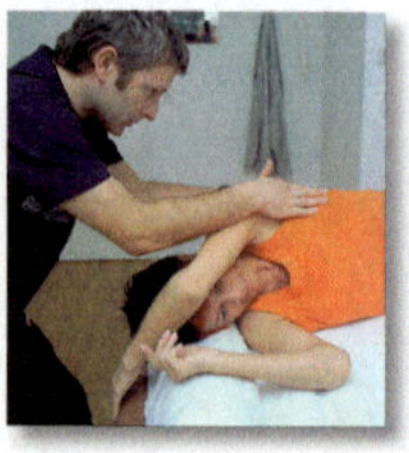

The phrases in the boxes will help you.

I'm (really) good at …
I'm interested in …
My favourite school subject is …
I enjoy/like … because …
I have already done work experience as a …
It was interesting/exciting/fun/boring/…
I would like to work as a … because …
I have always dreamt of becoming a …
What do you think?

As far as I know, you're (also) good at …
You enjoy/like …, don't you?
How did you like your work experience as a …?
I have already done work experience as a …
It was interesting/exciting/fun/boring/…
Have you ever thought about working as a …?
Perhaps you should become a …
Do you think that becoming a … would be right for you?
I think that you should …

The phrases in the boxes will help you.

I'm good at/interested in …
I enjoy/like …
I have already …
I would like to …
I have always dreamt of …
What do you …?

As far as I know …
You enjoy/like …, don't you?
How did you like …?
I have already …
Have you ever thought of …?
I think that you should …

LISTENING

Tipp

Schritt 1 – **Vor dem ersten Hören:** Lies die Aufgabe(n).
Schritt 2 – **Beim ersten Hören:** Bearbeite die Aufgabe(n).
Schritt 3 – **Beim zweiten Hören:** Vervollständige und verbessere deine Antworten.

Mr Goldman

a) Listen to Mr Goldman talking to some students. Match the sentence parts.

A	The students have already
B	Mr Goldman's father
C	Mr Goldman and his family
D	The Rubensteins

1	left Germany in 1938.
2	had family in New York.
3	read a book about Mr Goldman's life.
4	learned a lot about immigration.
5	had a shop in Berlin.

A	
B	
C	
D	

b) Read the sentence beginnings and endings. Tick ✓ the correct endings.

1. The class have talked about immigrants from …
   - A ☐ England and France.
   - B ☐ France and Germany.
   - C ☐ Great Britain and Ireland.
2. The film Rizwan saw was about Ireland …
   - A ☐ in the 18th century.
   - B ☐ in the 19th century.
   - C ☐ in the 20th century.
3. Mr Goldman and his family lived in …
   - A ☐ Berlin.
   - B ☐ Hamburg.
   - C ☐ Munich.
4. Mr Goldman came to the USA with …
   - A ☐ his parents and his two brothers.
   - B ☐ his parents and his grandmother.
   - C ☐ his parents and his sister.
5. Mr Goldman …
   - A ☐ is too old to remember the journey.
   - B ☐ was a little boy when he left Germany.
   - C ☐ would like to see Germany again one day.
6. The Rubensteins …
   - A ☐ came to the USA with the Goldmans.
   - B ☐ had already left Germany.
   - C ☐ helped the Goldmans find an apartment.

7. Mr Goldman and his family went to New York …

A ☐ by car.
B ☐ by ship.
C ☐ by plane.

8. They arrived in the United States …

A ☐ in the morning.
B ☐ in the evening.
C ☐ in the middle of the night.

c) Answer the questions in complete sentences.

1. Why have the class invited Mr Goldman?

____

____

2. When was Mr Goldman born?

____

3. Why did the Goldmans decide to leave Germany?

____

____

4. Who was Mrs Rubenstein?

____

5. How long did the journey to New York take?

____

6. What was uncomfortable about the journey to New York?

____

____

____

7. What was the first thing Mr Goldman saw when he arrived in America?

____

8. How did he feel when he arrived?

____

READING

Tipp

Schritt 1 – **Vor dem Lesen:** Sieh dir die **Überschrift** an und überlege, worum es gehen könnte. Lies die Aufgabe(n) und überlege, was gesucht ist.

Schritt 2 – **Beim Lesen: Unterstreiche** die Informationen, die für die Aufgabe(n) gesucht werden.

A German immigrant in the USA

Read the text about the famous architect John A. Roebling.

Johann August Röbling was born on 12 June 1806 in Mühlhausen, a small town in Germany. As a young boy, he liked listening to music, reading and painting. He also built a model bridge when he was only nine years old.

In 1824, Röbling's mother sent him to Berlin to study architecture[1] and engineering[2]. It was his dream to build bridges, but there weren't many bridge projects in Germany at the time. Röbling worked on a few of them and made plans for some bridges in Germany, but they were never built.

On 22 May 1831, Röbling left Germany with his brother Karl to go to America. They bought some land and Johann worked as a farmer, but he didn't like it, so he went back to being an architect after a few years.

In 1836, Röbling married Johanna Herting, who was also from Mühlhausen. Their son Washington, the first of nine children, was born in 1837. Röbling became an American citizen[3] in the same year and called himself John A. Roebling from that time on.

Roebling was always interested in suspension bridges[4] and worked on many bridge projects. Some of the bridges are even named after him, like the John A. Roebling Suspension Bridge over the Ohio River, which was the longest suspension bridge in the world until he designed his most famous bridge: the Brooklyn Bridge in New York.

Roebling started designing the Brooklyn Bridge in 1867. Two years later, he received a bad injury to his foot while working at the place where the bridge was later built. He became very ill and died in New York on 22 July 1869. The Brooklyn Bridge was finished by Roebling's son, Washington A. Roebling, and Washington's wife, Emily Warren Roebling. Emily learned about mathematics and engineering and helped her husband a lot at a time when women couldn't yet become engineers.

In 1883, the Brooklyn Bridge was finally finished. It had cost about $15.5 million. In today's money, that would be nearly $400 million. Emily Warren Roebling was the first person to walk across the Brooklyn Bridge on 24 May 1883.

John A. Roebling never knew that his bridge would one day become one of New York's most famous sights. Years after his death, it was discovered that the model bridge he had built as a nine-year-old looked very similar to his most important work: the Brooklyn Bridge.

1 *architecture* [ˈɑːkɪtɛktʃə]: Architektur
2 *engineering* [ˌɛndʒɪˈnɪərɪŋ]: Maschinenbau
3 *citizen* [ˈsɪtɪzn]: (Staats-)Bürger/in
4 *suspension bridge* [səsˈpɛnʃən brɪdʒ]: Hängebrücke

a) Match the sentence parts.

A	When John Roebling was a child, he	1	emigrated to America with his brother.	A	
B	Roebling's early bridge designs	2	began working on the Brooklyn Bridge.	B	
C	When he was nearly 25, Roebling	3	was the first person to cross the Brooklyn Bridge.	C	
D	Some of Roebling's American bridges	4	built his first bridge.	D	
E	At the age of 61, Roebling	5	were never realized.	E	
F	In 1883, Emily Warren Roebling	6	moved to Berlin to study.	F	
		7	are named after him.		

b) Read the sentence beginnings and endings. Tick ✓ the correct endings.

1. When Roebling was 18 years old, he …
   - A ☐ began to study in Berlin.
   - B ☐ moved to Erfurt.
   - C ☐ worked as a "Baumeister".
2. For Roebling it was difficult to find work in Germany because …
   - A ☐ his marks from university weren't very good.
   - B ☐ nobody liked his bridge designs.
   - C ☐ there wasn't much need for bridges.
3. In 1836, Roebling …
   - A ☐ founded a town in Pennsylvania.
   - B ☐ married Johanna Herting.
   - C ☐ went back to Mühlhausen.
4. After Roebling had become an American citizen …
   - A ☐ he changed his name.
   - B ☐ he worked as a farmer.
   - C ☐ his first child was born.
5. John A. Roebling died because …
   - A ☐ he fell off the Brooklyn Bridge.
   - B ☐ he injured his foot very badly at work.
   - C ☐ he worked too hard and didn't sleep enough.
6. After Roebling's death, work on the Brooklyn Bridge …
   - A ☐ stopped for fourteen years.
   - B ☐ was finished by his son and his son's wife.
   - C ☐ was organized by his wife Johanna Roebling.

c) Answer the questions in complete sentences.

1. What were Roebling's interests when he was a child?

2. What did Roebling do for some years after arriving in America?

3. What does the text say about Roebling's marriage and family in America?

4. What was special about the John A. Roebling Suspension Bridge?

5. What made Emily Warren Roebling's work special?

6. How long did it take to finish the Brooklyn Bridge after John A. Roebling's death?

7. How much did it cost to build the Brooklyn Bridge?

WRITING

Tipp

Schritt 1 – **Vor dem Schreiben:** Prüfe, ob der Text eine bestimmte Form haben muss (z. B. E-Mail). Lege den Inhalt und die Reihenfolge fest.
Schritt 2 – **Schreibe** deinen Text.
Schritt 3 – **Überarbeite** deinen Text: Kontrolliere zuerst, ob alle Inhalte vorkommen. Prüfe dann, ob es Grammatik- oder Rechtschreibfehler gibt. Verbessere sie.

○ My life as an exchange student

☆ **You have just returned home from a year as an exchange student in the USA. Write a blog entry about that year. Think about the following questions:**

- Where did you live? Who did you live with?
- What was your daily life like there?
- What did/didn't you like about living in the USA?
- How do you feel now that you're back home?

Write about 80 words. The ideas and phrases in the boxes will help you.

I lived in … with … • My American family was … • I (didn't) like … • After a while I felt … • I am going to miss …

go to high school • play sports • go sightseeing • make new friends • excited • scared • homesick • happy • …

Start like this: Hello everybody,

After a year in ____________, I am now back home. …

A natural disaster

Imagine there has been a flood in your home town. Your house has been badly damaged and you and your family will not be able to live there for a while.
Write a diary entry. Think about the following questions:

- Where are you and your family going to stay?
- What things can you take with you?
- What is going to happen to your pets?

- How do you feel about the situation?
- When do you think you will be able to go back to your home?

Write about 100 words. The ideas and phrases in the boxes will help you.

Last week … • We're going to stay with … • At the moment … • I think we will …

grandparents • friends • clothes • smartphone • books • scared • frightened • angry • hopeless • homesick • …

Start like this: Dear diary,

There has been a bad flood in our town. …

A new chance

Imagine you're an illegal immigrant in the USA. You and your parents left Mexico a few days ago and you have just arrived in Laredo, Texas, near the Mexican border. Write a letter to a friend and tell him/her about your journey. Think about the following questions:

- Why did you leave Mexico?
- How did you cross the border into the USA?

- How do you feel at this moment?
- What are you and your family going to do now?

Write about 120 words. The ideas in the box will help you.

no jobs • dangerous life • at night • run fast • excited • worried • scared • happy • find work • look for an apartment • …

Dear ____________,

I'm sorry I didn't tell you that we were leaving Mexico. We …

MEDIATION

Tipp

Gib in deinen eigenen Worten die **wichtigen Informationen** in der jeweils **anderen Sprache** wieder. Du musst **nicht Wort für Wort** übersetzen! Passe dabei deine Ausdrucksweise der Situation und den Sprecherinnen und Sprechern an.

José's story

You and your family are watching a documentary about illegal immigrants in the USA. Your parents are very interested in the topic, but the documentary is in English and they don't understand everything. Listen to José telling his story and answer your parents' questions.

1. Wo lebt José?

Er lebt in einer Stadt namens ______________________

2. Ist José ein illegaler Einwanderer?

Nein, er selbst ist ______________________

____

3. Welche Staatsangehörigkeit haben Josés Eltern?

Josés Eltern sind ______________________

4. Seit wann lebt Josés Familie in den Vereinigten Staaten?

Seine Eltern und Geschwister ______________________

____

5. Warum hat Josés Familie ihr Land verlassen?

Sie haben sich entschieden, zu gehen, weil ______________________

____

____

____

____

6. Wie ist Josés Familie über die Grenze in die USA gekommen?

Sie haben beschlossen, ______________________

____

7. Warum sind sie nachts über die Grenze gegangen?

Sie hatten gehört, dass ______________________________

____

____

8. Wann wurde denn José geboren?

José wurde ______________________________

9. Wie lebten José und seine Geschwister als Teenager?

Er sagt, dass sie ______________________________

____

10. Wo arbeiten Josés Eltern heute?

Sein Vater ______________________________

____

11. Wie ist Josés Leben in den USA jetzt?

José sagt, dass ______________________________

____

12. Wovor haben Josés Eltern und Geschwister Angst?

Sie haben immer Angst, ______________________________

____

13. Was ist Josés Vater vor einigen Monaten passiert?

Er wurde ______________________________

____

____

14. Wodurch könnte das Leben von Josés Familie in den USA erleichtert werden?

José meint, dass ______________________________

____

15. Warum denkt José, dass es für seine Familie wahrscheinlich erst einmal nicht einfacher wird?

Er sagt, dass viele ______________________________

____

WORDS AND GRAMMAR

Odd one out

Which word does not fit? Circle the odd one out.

1. sick • impossible • extreme • destroy
2. behind • once • in front • under
3. education • university • immigration • teacher
4. announce • emigrate • reach • pain
5. political • space • image • response
6. consider • opinion • escape • push

Definitions

Read the definitions. What are they? Write down the words.

1. to leave one country in order to live somewhere else: e _ _ _ _ _ _ _ _
2. another word for 'present': g _ _ _
3. words that explain or describe a picture or chart: c _ _ _ _ _ _
4. to get away from a dangerous situation: e _ _ _ _ _
5. a long trip: j _ _ _ _ _ _
6. a wish that something will happen: h _ _ _

What do the following words mean? Explain them in English.

1. war: ____________________
2. university: ____________________
3. racist: ____________________
____
4. government: ____________________
____
5. sick: ____________________
6. rent: ____________________
____

Word lists

a) Put the words in the correct lists. One of the word belongs in two lists.

destroy • extreme • impossible • emigrate • government • reach • racist • war • university • sick • political • announce • education • feed

people or things	what you can do	how things / people can be

b) Find two more words from *Theme 5* for each list.

c) Choose eight of the words in the lists and write a sentence with each of them.

___

___

___

___

___

___

___

___

___

___

___

A famous immigrant

Complete the sentences about Arnold Schwarzenegger. Circle the correct past perfect form.

1. When Arnold Schwarzenegger **finished / had finished** school in Austria[1], he joined the army[2].
2. After he **had left / has left** the army, he concentrated on sport.
3. Before Schwarzenegger went to the USA, he **had been winning / had won** several bodybuilding competitions in Austria.
4. After he **moves / had moved** to the USA, he began to work on his career there.
5. When he **had learned / learned** enough English, he took classes at university.
6. When Schwarzenegger **has lived / had lived** in the USA for 15 years, he became an American.

1 *Austria* [ˈɒstrɪə]: Österreich   2 *army* [ˈɑːmi]: Armee, Militär

Complete the sentences about Arnold Schwarzenegger with the correct forms of the verbs in brackets (). Decide whether to use the simple past or the past perfect.

1. Arnold Schwarzenegger had played (play) football for many years before he ______ (become) a bodybuilder.
2. When he ______ (do) bodybuilding for a while, he ______ (stop) playing football.
3. When Schwarzenegger ______ (win) the important 'Mr Universe' competition twice, his international career ______ (start).
4. After he ______ (end) his bodybuilding career, he ______ (decide) to become an actor.
5. After he ______ (play) some small roles on television, he ______ (become) a big Hollywood film star.
6. Schwarzenegger ______ (be) in a relationship with Maria Shriver for nearly nine years when they ______ (marry) in 1986.

Use the words in brackets () to join the two sentences about Arnold Schwarzenegger. Use the past perfect for the first action.

1. People saw some of Arnold Schwarzenegger's films. They accepted him as an actor. (after)

After people had

2. Schwarzenegger worked as an actor for many years. He went into politics[1]. (after)

3. He won the election[2] to become Governor[3] of California in 2006. He tried to do good things for nature. (when)

4. He announced that he wanted to make films again. He ended his career in politics. (before)

5. He tested if his fans still liked him. He acted in a big film project again. (before)

6. Schwarzenegger and Maria Shriver were married for 25 years. They broke up. (after)

1 *politics* ['pɒlətɪks]: Politik
2 *election* [ɪ'lɛkʃn]: Wahl
3 *Governor* ['gʌvənə]: Gouverneur/in

Before and after

Complete the sentences with the past perfect forms of the verbs in brackets ().

1. Before the Europeans came, only Native Americans ______ (live) in North America.

2. After many people ______ (die) in the potato famine, lots of Irish people emigrated to the USA.

3. When the new immigration station at Ellis Island ______ (open), all the new immigrants had to pass through it.

4. Before they arrived at Ellis Island, people ______ (spend) weeks on ships.

5. When immigration officers and doctors ______ (check) them, the immigrants were allowed to go to New York.

6. After the immigrants ______ (find) somewhere to live, they built a new life for themselves in the USA.

Complete the sentences with the correct forms of the verbs in brackets (). Decide whether you have to use the simple past or the past perfect.

1. After Jessica had finished (finish) school,

she ______ (work) in England for a year.

2. Before she ______ (decide) to go abroad,

she ______ (talk) to her family and friends about it.

3. When she ______ (think) about everything for a while,

she ______ (apply) for a student job.

4. After she ______ (take) a language test,

she ______ (go) to England for a job interview.

5. When she ______ (do) some training,

she ______ (start) her new job.

6. After she ______ (spend) a year in England,

she ______ (speak) English very well.

Use the words in brackets () to join the two actions. Use the past perfect for the first action.

1. The government warned the people. The hurricane hit the town. (before)

The government had

2. The people bought lots of food and water. The storm arrived. (before)

3. The storm destroyed their homes. The people built new houses. (after)

4. The people in Syria lived normal lives. The war began. (before)

5. Their homes were destroyed in the war. Many people went to Europe. (after)

6. They found new homes in Europe. They tried to start a new life. (when)

SPEAKING

◯ A new life

Tipp

Beschreibe das Bild so genau wie möglich. Sage, was du an welchen Stellen im Bild siehst.

☆ ☾ ☼ **Look at the picture and talk about it.**

☆ ☾ **Talk about the following questions. The words and phrases in the boxes will help you.**

- What can you see?
- Where are the people in the picture?
- Who are the people? Where are they from?
- How do they feel?

☆

I can see … • There is/are … • on the left/right • in the centre/foreground/background • The people are … • They have got … • Perhaps they are … • I think …

train station • bag • teddy bear • tired • nervous • happy • excited • …

☾

I can see … • There is/are … • on the left/right • in the centre/foreground/background • The people are … • They have got … • Perhaps they are … • I think …

☼ **Talk about the following questions.**

- What can you see?
- Where are the people in the picture?
- Who are the people? Where are they from?
- Try to imagine how you would feel in their situation. What would make you happy/sad? What would you miss most?

Lösungen

THEME 1: Welcome to the USA

S. 6 – 7 Listening: Let's talk about food

a) The school project is about typical American food.

b) Karen: B cornflakes, L a salad, D rice with vegetables
Jacques: B a bagel, L a turkey sandwich, D Chinese food
Dennis: B pancakes, L a cheese sandwich, D pasta with cheese

c) 1. A 2. C 3. C 4. A 5. C 6. A

d) 1. She doesn't like fast food because she prefers fresh, healthy food.
2. She thinks it is important to take the time to cook, sit down and eat.
3. Jacques thinks that typical American food is burgers, hot dogs and steaks.
4. He thinks the food in New York is special because there's food from so many different countries.
5. She says it is the most important meal of the day.
6. Sometimes she makes meat loaf, and for Thanksgiving she makes turkey.

S. 8 – 10 Reading: Secret sights in New York City

a) A A building with a history
B A garden in the city
C Treasures from the garbage
D A special place to look at pictures

b) 1. right
2. wrong
3. right
4. right
5. right
6. wrong
7. wrong
8. right

c) 2. Between 1856 and 1875, about 7,000 patients came to the hospital every year.
6. It is organized by size and colour.
7. Street art in the Freedom Tunnel began in 1974.

d) 1. Roosevelt Island is in the East River between Manhattan and Queens.
2. It was built away from the city centre to keep the illness away from healthy people.
3. It was used as a school for nurses and closed in the 1950s.
4. You can visit all year round.
5. It started because he wanted to make his corner of the garage at work a little prettier.
6. The pieces are found by Molina and the other workers.
7. After the tunnel was closed, homeless people began to live there and street artists came.

S. 11 Writing: My neighbourhood

Lösungsvorschlag:
I live in Frankfurt. It's a big city in Germany. I live in a house with my parents, my brother and my sister. We live near my school, so I don't have to get up too early in the morning. My neighbourhood is nice and quiet and a lot of families live there. What I don't like is that most of my friends don't live here, so it's a little boring sometimes. My favourite place is the park. I often go there after school or at weekends.

S. 12 Writing: A travel guide

Lösungsvorschlag:
A day in Cologne!
If you come to Cologne, you really must visit Cologne Cathedral first. It's our most famous sight and I promise you'll love it. Go to the top of one of the towers and enjoy a great view! If you're interested in history or art, you can choose from many museums. Families love Cologne Zoo, especially on sunny days. Go and visit the elephants! If you've still got time, just take a walk round the city centre and try one of the many fantastic cafés and restaurants, or take a boat trip on the Rhine. Cologne is also great for shopping – there really is something for everyone here!

S. 13 Writing: A day in New York City

Lösungsvorschlag:
Dear Mum and Dad,
What a day! We got up early this morning and took the ferry to Liberty Island to see the Statue of Liberty. After that, we went to Ellis Island, where millions of immigrants arrived when they first came to the USA. Later, we had a picnic lunch in Central Park and relaxed a little. In the afternoon, we walked around the city and saw many famous sights, like the Flatiron Building and Times Square. Tomorrow, we're going to go to an art museum first. That sounds a little boring, but Tim's parents really want to go. And maybe we'll look at the shops on 5th Avenue …

I'm really tired now. Have a good night and see you soon!
Love,
Kathy

S. 14 – 15 Mediation: Holiday food in the USA

Lösungsvorschlag:

1. My mum would like to know what Americans usually eat at Christmas.
2. Sie essen zum Erntedankfest und zu Weihnachten normalerweise Truthahn. Zum Nachtisch gibt es oft einen Pie, zum Beispiel Apfel oder Kürbis.
3. Robert möchte wissen, was wir in Deutschland an Weihnachten essen.
4. We like to eat fish, but many families eat potato salad and sausages. There is no traditional dish that all Germans eat at Christmas.
5. She asks what side dish you have with the turkey.
6. Es gibt meistens Gemüse, also Brokkoli, Möhren oder Bohnen, und natürlich Kartoffeln.

Lösungsvorschlag:

7. My mum says that everything is delicious. She'd like to know why the potatoes are orange.
8. Robert sagt, dass das keine normalen Kartoffeln sind, sondern Süßkartoffeln. Die essen sie oft an Feiertagen.
9. She says that she doesn't really know what Americans usually eat – she only knows hamburgers and hot dogs.
10. Cathy isst gern Salat. Die Kinder mögen Obst, also gehen sie oft zum Bauernmarkt, um frisches Obst und Gemüse zu kaufen.
11. Robert mag Fast Food oder traditionelle Gerichte wie zum Beispiel Hackbraten, aber Cathy möchte, dass er gesund isst, also gibt es nicht oft Hamburger oder Hot Dogs.

Lösungsvorschlag:

12. In Germany, Italian and Chinese restaurants are very popular. My mum asks if that's similar here.
13. Cathy sagt, dass es hier viele verschiedene Restaurants gibt. Sie mögen italienisches, mexikanisches und chinesisches Essen.
14. She says that the meal was wonderful. She'd like to cook a German dish for you tomorrow.

S. 16 – 17 Words and Grammar: Words, words, words

1. capital
2. settler
3. step
4. skill
5. impression
6. south

1. states
2. inhabitants
3. floors
4. busy
5. languages
6. review
7. flat
8. imagine

Lösungsvorschlag:

1. background: where a person is from
2. centre: the middle of something
3. community: a group of people who share something, for example their religion
4. complain: to say that you don't like something
5. enjoy oneself: to like what you are doing
6. fact file: a text with information about a person or thing
7. immigrant: someone who comes to a country because he or she wants to live there
8. study: to learn about something

S. 17 Words and Grammar: Phrases

A3 B1 C7 D6 E4 F5

1. learn a new skill for life
2. give a history presentation
3. be a new immigrant
4. live in a big flat
5. support a sports team
6. a busy city centre
7. take place on Wednesday afternoon
8. imagine an exciting story

S. 18 Words and Grammar: American English

Lösungsvorschlag:

high school, cab, downtown, schedule, elevator, sneaker, washroom, movie

S. 18 – 19 Words and Grammar: Reflexive pronouns

a) I → myself
you → yourself
he → himself
she → herself
it → itself
we → ourselves
you → yourselves
they → themselves

b) 1. Tom, look at yourself! Your face is dirty!
2. I can't look at myself. I hate my new haircut.
3. Our football team has won! The players should be proud of themselves.

4. Sarah is really nervous about the test on Friday. She should believe in herself.
5. I have to take a look at my bike this weekend. It's not going to repair itself!
6. I am sure you will enjoy yourselves at the match.

1. My finger hurts a little. I cut myself with a knife earlier.
2. Sam and Tom, you should believe in yourselves. I'm sure you'll win.
3. They didn't collect the money for themselves – it was for a charity.
4. Our dog can look after himself for a few hours. He'll probably just sleep.
5. I sometimes talk to myself when my homework is difficult.
6. Our holiday was great! We really enjoyed ourselves.
7. Jane taught herself a bit of Spanish before her trip.

1. "My computer keeps turning itself off. I don't know what's wrong." – "Don't worry, I'll help you. I'm sure we can repair it together."
2. Annie hurt herself when she cleaned the windows. Luckily her sister was there to help her.
3. Excuse me, we're lost. Could you please tell us how to get to the Empire State Building?
4. Zachary is good at maths, but he needs to believe in himself more. I think you should talk to him.
5. I'm rather angry with myself. I forgot to return some books to the library yesterday.
6. Mum, we're old enough to look after ourselves at home. Have fun at the cinema!
7. Tara and Alan are really enjoying themselves in New York. I know because they called me yesterday.

S. 20 – 21 Words and Grammar: Shopping for clothes

Mother: OK, let's start. What about a sweater – do you need a new one?
Kevin: I guess I do. But I don't like these white sweaters here – I prefer dark ones.
Mother: Here are some grey sweaters … and there are some blue ones over there.
Kevin: Can I have a dark blue one?
Mother: Sure! Try this one on. It's a large.
Kevin: I think that's the right size. Hey, there are some cool sweaters in that corner!
Mother: What, the ones by the door? They're really expensive – £65!

Father: We really need to buy some new clothes for you. The ones you have are too small now. Let's see. There are a lot of shops to choose from. This one looks interesting.
Pete: OK.
Father: Wonderful! Come on. You need some new T-shirts. Your old ones look terrible.
Pete: I like the ones in that corner over there.
Father: Try them on, then. OK, jackets are over there. Would you like a blue one or a black one?
Pete: I'd prefer green.
Father: Well, you can try this one on then. Look, there are some pullovers by the window. I think you could use some new ones.
Pete: I don't like the ones they have here. Let's try a different shop.

Lelaina: I think I need some new shoes. All my old ones don't look good anymore.
Mother: What about the ones you bought last month?
Lelaina: I don't like them anymore. They make my feet hurt.
Mother: Well, OK. What about dresses?
Lelaina: I saw some nice ones in a shop down the road.
Mother: What about this one right here? Look, it's your size.
Lelaina: I don't really like the colour. But I'd also like a new skirt. Have you seen the one that Annie bought last week? It looks fantastic!
Mother: No, I haven't. Why don't you try this one on?
Lelaina: I prefer the ones in the shop next door. They've also got cool scarves. I want to look at the one in the shop window. Annie has got the same one.
Mother: OK, I give up. Let's go next door then.

S. 21 – 22 Words and Grammar: Some or any?

1. Mum, can you give me some money? I need it for lunch.
2. Zach can't find his jacket anywhere. He must have left it at school.
3. I'm sorry, but we can't have pancakes – I haven't got any eggs.
4. John, can you come over here? I think I saw someone in the garden.
5. It's Fiona's birthday next week, but I can't think of anything to get her.
6. Sarah, you haven't had a real holiday in a long time. You should go somewhere nice this summer.

1. There are some interesting articles in today's newspaper.
2. I can't find my sandwich. I'm sure somebody has eaten it.
3. Has anybody seen Dave today? Is he ill?
4. Mum, I want to go to the party tomorrow, but I haven't got anything to wear!
5. Can we go to Washington, D.C. next weekend? I haven't been anywhere this year yet.
6. Welcome, Mrs Henderson! Would you like something to drink?
7. I don't know what to do on my birthday. I really haven't got any ideas.
8. Lucy must be somewhere around here. I saw her only a minute ago.

1. Can you help me? I think there's <u>something</u> in my left eye.
2. Julie, there's <u>somebody</u> at the door. Can you go and look, please?
3. Justin is new in town – he doesn't really know <u>anybody</u> yet.
4. Do you live <u>anywhere</u> near Sandy? Somebody should take her today's homework.
5. It's really hot in here. I need <u>something</u> to drink.
6. Do you know if Frank is ill? – Sorry, but I don't know <u>anything</u> about why he isn't here.
7. I really like fruit, but I can't find <u>any</u> apples.
8. Look in the kitchen. I think you will find <u>some</u> in there.

S. 23 Speaking: My favourite sports

Lösungsvorschlag:
My favourite sport is baseball. You play it in a team and there are nine players in each team. You have to throw a ball and a player from the other team tries to hit it far away with his or her bat. The player who has hit the ball tries to run around the field before the other team has the ball. I like baseball because you play it outside, so you get a lot of fresh air. You can play baseball with your friends and that is a lot of fun. I play on my school team and we practise every Monday and Thursday from 3 pm to 5 pm.
I would also like to try field hockey. I think that is a lot of fun too, and I really like team sports.

THEME 2: Challenges

S. 24 – 25 Listening: My biggest challenge

a) Tom: 5 Pamela: 1
Jenny: 4 James: 3

b) 1. wrong 5. wrong
2. right 6. right
3. right 7. right
4. right 8. wrong

c) 1. They have a big garden where they grow fruit and vegetables.
5. Pamela can't even stand on chairs to hang a picture.
8. James never wants to smoke again.

d) 1. People love them because they are organic.
2. He is proud of his father because he is trying very hard to find a job.
3. Jenny's grandmother lives around the corner from Jenny.
4. She is happy because, thanks to Jenny's help, she can still live in her own apartment.
5. Pamela was very proud of herself and the others.
6. James quit smoking two months ago.
7. James started smoking because he thought it was cool. He wanted to be part of a group and he felt accepted by them when he smoked.

S. 26 – 28 Reading: Working hard makes winning feel better

a) Being successful feels even better when you've had to work for it.

b) 1. wrong 6. wrong
2. right 7. wrong
3. wrong 8. right
4. right 9. right
5. right 10. right

c) 1. Janet has been doing track and field since she was six.
3. She wasn't famous, but people knew who she was.
6. She broke her leg six weeks later when she was playing basketball.
7. Janet had to stay in hospital for ten days.

d) 1. They knew about her because she was successful and there were articles about her in the local newspaper.
2. She was very sad about it and it was difficult for her to deal with the situation. She decided to train

even harder after some of her friends had made fun of her, but then she had the accident.
3. She was angry because they were fit and she wasn't.
4. They went for walks in the park with her as soon as she was able to.
5. Kelly went swimming with Janet to make her leg strong again.
6. She started training again in the spring and after about two months, she was able to practise three or four times a week again.
7. Janet is no longer upset when Kelly wins.
8. She has learned not to give up. Janet thinks that winning feels even better when you've had to work hard for it.

S. 29 Writing: Halima's biggest challenge

☆ *Lösungsvorschlag:*

When I was 14 years old, I started smoking. My friends were smokers and I wanted to be part of the group. I soon smoked a lot and I felt stressed and unhealthy all the time. My parents were angry with me, too. I tried to quit, but it's hard to do that alone. I finally joined a group of people who wanted to quit smoking and we helped each other. I don't smoke anymore and I feel happy and healthy now.

S. 30 Writing: Christopher's biggest challenge

☾ *Lösungsvorschlag:*

My biggest challenge was running a 10-kilometre race to raise money for charity. I really don't enjoy running, but I wanted to do it because my sister works for a children's charity and they always need money. I trained with my best friend and we went running several times a week. Many of my friends and family agreed to give money to the charity if I managed to finish the race. And I did! I was very tired, but really proud of myself in the end.

S. 31 Writing: Their biggest challenge

☼ *Lösungsvorschlag:*

My biggest challenge was taking care of my grandparents for three months. Last year, my grandfather fell and broke his arm, and a few weeks later my grandmother broke her leg when she had an accident riding her bike. They needed help with everything: getting dressed, shopping, cooking, cleaning the house … My parents did what they could, but both have a job. I did all the shopping for my grandparents and cooked their dinner every evening. It was difficult because I had to do everything after school and I also had football practice three times a week, but it was important to me to help them. They have always been there for me. They're much better now, and the experience has brought us even closer together

S. 32 – 33 Mediation: A support group

☆ ☾ ☼ *Lösungsvorschlag:*

1. Das ist Phil. Er fragt, ob du hier bist, um mich zu besuchen.
2. Hartmut says that he is visiting my family. My mother is his sister.
3. He says that I have told him about this support group. He also wants to change something and quit smoking.
4. Jack erzählt, dass seine Freundin sauer auf ihn war, weil er immer nach Rauch gerochen hat.
5. Das ist Alison. Sie findet, dass es genau richtig ist, zu einer solchen Gruppe zu gehen. Ihr hat das wirklich geholfen.

☾ ☼ *Lösungsvorschlag:*

6. He says that is good. He's always tired and he hasn't got any energy.
7. Hartmut would like to know how you quit smoking.
8. Alison sagt, dass sie versucht hat, weniger zu rauchen. Sie hat in der ersten Woche 20 Zigaretten geraucht, in der zweiten nur noch zehn. Sie hat auch Nikotinkaugummi gekaut.
9. Phil erzählt, dass er erst sehr müde war und immer rauchen wollte. Aber nach ein paar Wochen war er schon fitter, konnte länger rennen und hat mehr Dinge unternommen, die Spaß machen.

☼ *Lösungsvorschlag:*

10. Hartmut thinks that sounds good. He says he should do more sport – he likes to go swimming, for example.
11. Jack sagt, dass viele etwas zunehmen, wenn sie mit dem Rauchen aufhören. Es hilft, sich gesund zu ernähren. Er probiert gern neue Rezepte aus.
12. Hartmut says thank you. He wants to try that, and he wants to join a support group back home. He is sure that it's easier if people support each other.

S. 34 Words and Grammar: Phrases

☆ A3 B5 C6 D7 E1 F2

☾ ☼ a) 1. face a difficult problem
2. climb a high mountain
3. be proud of winning a race
4. advise a friend to quit smoking

5. get angry quickly
6. seem like a nice person
7. hurt yourself in an accident
8. leave rubbish around

b) *Lösungsvorschlag:*
1. If you're facing a difficult problem, it's often a good idea to ask for help.
2. I wouldn't like to climb a high mountain – I'd be scared.
3. My sister was proud of winning a race for charity.
4. Zoe advised her friend Tanya to quit smoking.
5. Henry gets angry quickly – I think he should work on that.
6. Our new teacher really seems like a nice person.
7. Last year my mum hurt herself in a car accident.
8. When you have a picnic in the park, you mustn't leave any rubbish around.

S. 35 Words and Grammar: Crosswords

1. climb
2. cigarette
3. seem
4. skin
5. energy
6. store

solution word: challenge

1. smoke
2. face
3. courage
4. youth
5. top
6. attractive
7. right

S. 36 Words and Grammar: Explain

1. resident: someone who lives in a building or a place
2. courage: If you have this, you are not afraid
3. to advise somebody: to tell somebody what (not) to do, what would be best
4. challenge: a difficult situation that tests your courage or strength
5. sheet: a piece of paper
6. to remove: to take something away from a place

S. 36 – 37 Words and Grammar: What do you enjoy doing?

Ben: Playing the guitar is my favourite activity. I love practising with my band. I think being in a band is really cool. All the girls love it!
Gail: I prefer sports. Swimming keeps me fit. I love going to the pool in the afternoon. Of course I always enjoy winning competitions.
Ben: I think it's important to have a hobby, but getting good marks at school is also important – even though I hate doing my homework.

Ben: I like spending time with my band. We enjoy writing songs together and I really like trying different instruments.
Gail: My friends and I often meet after school. We enjoy just relaxing in the park together or listening to loud music. At weekends, we like to go dancing at the youth club together – they often have good parties there.
Ben: I like visiting my grandma on Sundays. Eating home-made waffles or cake is not a bad way to spend an afternoon!

Ben: I agree. I really don't like having breakfast alone. My mum has to leave for work early, so I'm all by myself at breakfast time.
Gail: I have to say I really enjoy walking to school. When it's raining, I go by bus, but I hate taking the bus. You never get a seat.
Ben: I know what you mean, but waiting in line at lunchtime is really bad, too. It takes forever to get your food.
Gail: You know, I just love coming home to a nice cup of tea and some biscuits. My mum and I always talk a little before I do my homework.
Ben: That's really nice. My parents and I always cook dinner together. I think helping at home is important. Tidying the living room is my job.
Gail: I also have to help a little, but that's OK. I like feeding the dog, for example.

S. 38 – 40 Words and Grammar: Tell me what to do

1. Coach Miller told us to run as fast as possible with the ball.
2. He told us to watch the players in the other team.
3. Coach Miller told us not to let the other team score too many points.
4. He told us to drink lots of water during the breaks.
5. He told us not to be late for the second half of the game.
6. He told us to enjoy the game.

1. My mother told me to mix the butter and sugar in a big bowl.
2. She told me to add the eggs, flour and milk slowly.
3. She advised me not to bake the cake for more than 60 minutes.
4. My mother told me to take the cake out and let it cool for an hour.
5. She told me not to touch the hot oven.

6. She told me to prepare some fresh cream for the cake.
7. My mother advised me to put chocolate or fruit on top of the cream.
8. She advised me not to put the candles on the cake too soon.

1. Melissa's father asked her to take out the rubbish.
2. Tim and Kathy's parents told them to tidy the living room.
3. Elena's mother told her to clean her rabbits' cage.
4. Zoe and Kyle's grandfather asked them to find his reading glasses for him.
5. David's father told him not to leave his dirty plate on the table.
6. Anne and Henry's grandparents asked them not to eat cake in their bedrooms.
7. Andy's parents told him not to forget his grandmother's birthday.
8. Becca's mother asked her to repair her bike before school the next day.

S. 40 – 42 Words and Grammar: What have you been doing?

1. Tom has been doing judo since he was eight years old.
2. I have been working on my history presentation since 3 pm.
3. Richard has been waiting for his food for nearly an hour.
4. Jessica and her friends have been playing Monopoly for six hours.
5. You have been driving for four hours. Let's take a break.
6. Jill and Rita's parents have been watching them play for a while.

1. Alex has been sleeping all afternoon. Is he ill?
2. My grandfather has been taking driving lessons since August.
3. Sally and Jonas haven't been going out for long, but they're very happy together.
4. Dad has been reading since this morning. His new book must be good.
5. Chris has been practising for this concert for weeks. He's really good now.
6. Gerald has been working here since 2005. He likes his job.
7. Fred hasn't been learning German for long, but he's already quite good.
8. Sheila's grandparents have been travelling around the world for six months.

1. Have you been working here for long?
– Yes, I have. For nearly ten years now.
2. Has Joe been sitting there since this morning?
– No, he hasn't. He has just come in from the garden.
3. Have the children been watching TV for long?
– No, they haven't. They have just come home from school.
4. Has Linda been helping you with your homework?
– Yes, she has. She has explained everything to me.
5. How long has Gemma been trying to repair her car?
– I'm not sure, but she seems to know what the problem is now.
6. What have you been doing all morning?
– I have been in the park with some friends. Sorry, have you been looking for me?
7. How long has dad been tidying up the house?
– For about three hours, but he's finished now. I feel bad – I should have helped him.
8. How long has Jack been learning for his maths test?
– For a week, I think. He should believe in himself more – I know he's good at maths.

S. 42 – 43 Words and Grammar: The passive

1. Karen has been chosen to represent her school in the town championships. She is very proud.
2. Many different languages are spoken in America.
3. Jim's car was stolen in New York. He was very upset about it.
4. Land diving is done by young men on Vanuatu to show their courage.
5. The big tree in our garden is very old. It is going to be cut down by our gardener.
6. I would like to go to the football match, but all the tickets have been sold.

1. These messages were left for you today. At least two are from grandma.
2. My grandparents' house was built in 1997. It's very nice and quite modern.
3. The hamsters were fed an hour ago. They don't need any food now.
4. Natalie's birthday cake was made by her best friends Ashley and Hannah.

5. These pictures were taken during our holiday in Peru. We had a great time there.
6. This book was published last month. I think you'll like it – it's great!

☼ 1. Some beautiful flowers have been sent to Lydia.
2. The rent will be collected next week.
3. Nearly £2,000 was raised for a local charity last weekend.
4. Graffiti has been sprayed on one of the school walls.
5. A tower for land diving is built in the village every year.
6. Many different kinds of vegetable are sold at the local farmers' market.

S. 44 – 45 Speaking: Facing a challenge
☆ ☾ ☼ *Lösungsvorschlag:*
A: Hello, B. I'm really proud of myself right now – I have dealt with a really difficult challenge.
B: Hello, A! That sounds great – what was the challenge?
A: I helped to build a house for poor people during the summer holidays.
B: That sounds great! What was difficult about the challenge?
A: It was difficult because it was a lot of hard work and I had to do it during my free time.
B: How did you feel during that time?
A: I was often tired in the evenings and I wasn't always sure I could do it. But every evening, I felt really good about myself.
B: What helped you to deal with everything?
A: I really wanted to do something for other people. I've got a nice life and I wanted to give something back. That helped me a lot.
B: How did you feel afterwards?
A: I was even more tired after everything was finished, but I felt really proud. I helped to make sure that lots of people now have a place to sleep and eat. That feels great!
B: What have you learned from the experience?
A: I have learned that I am much stronger than I thought. It's good to remember why you're doing something and to keep going – nothing has ever felt better than that!

THEME 3: Love and friendship

S. 46 – 47 Listening: *West Side Story*
☆ ☾ ☼ a) classroom

b) 1. B 2. A 3. B 4. C 5. B 6 B

☾ ☼ c) A7 B1 C4 D9 E3 F8 G5 H6

☼ d) 1. Work on *West Side Story* began in 1949.
2. The Tony Awards are like the Oscars, but for theatre.
3. The film won the Oscars for the Best Film and the Best Music.
4. There are 18 songs in *West Side Story*.
5. The Community Drama Club will give ten performances.
6. Teresa thinks that the story is fantastic.

S. 48 – 50 Reading: Four true love stories
☆ ☾ ☼ a) A No happy ending
B A Hollywood romance
C A king no more
D A real-life princess

b)	A	B	C	D
1.		✓		
2.		✓	✓	
3.			✓	
4.			✓	✓
5.	✓			
6.	✓			

☾ ☼ c) 1. Evita grew up very poor.
2. Richard Burton and Elizabeth Taylor acted together in many Hollywood films.
3. Wallis Simpson was American.
4. Prince Rainier died in 2005 and Princess Grace died in 1982.

☼ d) 1. The story of Juan and Evita Perón ended tragically because Evita died when she was very young.
2. Richard Burton and Elizabeth Taylor met when they both had roles in the film *Cleopatra*.
3. Richard Burton and Elizabeth Taylor were married for ten years before they broke up.
4. Edward VIII wanted to marry Wallis Simpson, but as king, he was not allowed to. He chose love.
5. Grace Kelly was a successful actress before she married Prince Rainier.
6. Princess Grace died in a car accident at the age of 52. Prince Rainier never married again.

S. 51 Writing: The perfect friend

Lösungsvorschlag:

I think a perfect friend is someone who is funny and likes to do sport. It would be great if (s)he was good at playing football, so we could do that together. We could also relax and listen to music or watch films together. My perfect friend would also be good at school and help me with my homework. I want my friend to be there for me when I need him/her and I want him/her to keep our secrets.

S. 52 Writing: *Romeo and Juliet* – like or dislike?

Lösungsvorschlag:

Romeo and Juliet is a famous play by William Shakespeare about two lovers who cannot be together because their families are enemies. In the end, they both kill themselves. I didn't like the story because it is very sad and because I think it is quite unrealistic. Romeo and Juliet have only just met, but they're already in love and want to marry. One thing I didn't like either was the fact that Juliet still wants to be with Romeo after he has killed her cousin. I think the ending is much too dramatic: Juliet wakes up just in time to see Romeo die. I don't really like unrealistic stories like that.

S. 53 Writing: Your *Romeo and Juliet*

Lösungsvorschlag:

Romeo: Juliet! Juliet? Oh no! Is she dead? Juliet, please wake up! Wake up! I cannot live without you, my Juliet!

Juliet: (slowly) Romeo?

Romeo: Juliet! You aren't dead. Thank God! Come on, let's go! We can't stay here! We must be quick!

Juliet: I have a letter for my parents. I must give it to them – it will explain everything. Perhaps it will help to finally stop the fighting. Perhaps we will even be able to come home one day!

Romeo: No, that's too dangerous. Let's give your letter to Friar Laurence. He can give it to your parents after we have left. Come on, let's go. I can't wait to spend the rest of my life with you.

S. 54 – 56 Mediation: At the theatre

Lösungsvorschlag:

1. Stehplätze kosten 4 Pfund, Sitzplätze zwischen 20 und 45 Pfund.
2. Ja, die Sitzplätze gibt es für unter 18-Jährige je 4 Pfund günstiger.
3. Das Stück dauert etwa 2 Stunden und 45 Minuten. Es gibt aber auch eine Pause von 20 Minuten.

Lösungsvorschlag:

4. Es geht um zwei reiche Familien, die verfeindet sind. Ihre Kinder verlieben sich aber trotzdem ineinander.
5. Sie ist eher modern. Die Musik ist gemischt – sowohl klassische Musik als auch Popmusik. Außerdem werden auch Lichteffekte und Schusswaffen benutzt.
6. Der Hauptdarsteller heißt Nathaniel Williams und die Juliet wird von einer Jane Johnson gespielt. Ich kenne die beiden nicht.

Lösungsvorschlag:

7. Es gibt auf der Website mehrere Meinungen zu dem Stück. Frances Gilbert zum Beispiel schreibt, dass sie das Stück großartig fand, vor allem die Schauspielerinnen und Schauspieler. Die Musik hat ihr auch sehr gefallen. Kyle Ringrose meint, dass er das Stück sogar zwei Mal gesehen hat und es ihm sehr gefallen hat. Die Kostüme und Darsteller fand er toll und am Ende musste er weinen.
Allerdings ist Edward Thompson der Meinung, dass das Stück schrecklich ist. Für ihn hat die moderne Fassung alles ruiniert und er würde am liebsten sein Geld zurückverlangen.
Ich glaube, wir müssen einfach selbst herausfinden, ob es uns gefällt.

S. 57 Words and Grammar: Definitions

A5 B6 C7 D3 E2 F1

S. 57 Words and Grammar: Verbs, verbs, verbs

1. grow
2. admit
3. stare
4. lead
5. pass
6. notice
7. disappear

solution word: friendship

S. 58 Words and Grammar: Opposites

1. none
2. stupid
3. death
4. lead
5. love
6. dangerous
7. lose
8. enemy

S. 58 Words and Grammar: Phrases

A6 B3 C1 D5 E2 F7

S. 58 Words and Grammar: More words

1. date
2. grow
3. disappeared
4. lead
5. conversation
6. fight

S. 59 Words and Grammar: Some chat-up lines

Lösungsvorschlag:

1. Kiss me if I'm wrong but dinosaurs still exist, right?
2. Are you a magician? Because when I look at you, everyone else disappears.
3. I didn't know that angels really come to Earth.
4. We are not socks, but we would make a great pair.
5. Do I know you? You look exactly like my next girlfriend.

S. 59 – 61 Words and Grammar: Send me an email

1. Mary often sends her friends emails.
2. I usually take my grandfather some chocolate when I visit him.
3. Lisa made her boyfriend a beautiful card for Valentine's Day.
4. Ayla gave her brother a cool CD for his birthday.
5. Timothy showed his friends a picture of his girlfriend on his mobile.
6. After the holidays Rohit asked his classmates lots of questions.
7. Ciara buys her family and friends little presents whenever she's on holiday.

1. Liam sends his friends more than 100 messages every day.
2. Robbie promised his girlfriend a ring.
3. Aisha always gives her best friend money.
4. Ria gave her friend her English book.
5. Jason always gives his friend Sarah his English homework.
6. Naomi always takes her friends something sweet from her parents' shop.
7. Lynn gives her grandfather a little present every time she visits him.

1. Eliza writes her friends a lot of letters.
2. Greg told Bert a funny story.
3. Peter made his girlfriend a mixed CD for Valentine's Day.
4. Jamie bought Oliver a big birthday present.
5. Raj showed his friends photos of his trip to India.
6. His parents asked Neil a lot of questions about his new girlfriend.
7. Layla's grandmother sent Layla a present.

S. 62 Words and Grammar: In Verona

1. The Capulets and the Montagues talk proudly about themselves.
2. At first, Romeo and Juliet only look at each other shyly.
3. Romeo and Juliet speak quietly because they don't want to be heard.
4. When her father tells Juliet that she must marry Count Paris, she looks at him sadly.
5. When Juliet wakes up, she knows that her plan has not gone well.

1. The Capulets and the Montagues fight each other openly.
2. When Juliet arrives at the party, she smiles happily.
3. When Romeo sees Juliet, he falls madly in love with her.
4. Tybalt hurts Mercutio so severely that Mercutio dies.
5. Juliet goes to Friar Laurence secretly and talks to him.
6. When Juliet wakes up, she opens her eyes slowly.

1. Benvolio easily convinces Romeo to go to the ball.
2. When Romeo sees Juliet, he thinks she is incredibly beautiful.
3. Tybalt and Romeo fight angrily.
4. Romeo must leave Verona fast.
5. Friar Laurence thinks the love story of Romeo and Juliet will end happily.
6. However, the story ends badly for the young lovers.

S. 63 Words and Grammar: More than ever

1. I have never seen Lisa look at anyone more coldly than at her ex-boyfriend.
2. When Akello is with his new best friend, he talks more loudly than ever.
3. Matilda has never cried more terribly than when Mark left her.
4. When Julia is with Ruben, she speaks more nervously than usual.
5. Kojo tried harder than ever before to be nice to his new girlfriend's parents.
6. The next time Leroy helps him, Paolo should thank him more gratefully.

1. Breaking up with Lee was hard for Faye, but she can talk about it more easily now.
2. Ebo's new girlfriend is good for him. He even plays football better than before.
3. Callum smiles at his girlfriend more happily than ever before.
4. Leila got a few bad marks in maths, so she does her homework more carefully now.

5. Since Mika met Joy, he has been going to the gym and eating much more healthily.
6. Ahmet had never spoken more shyly than when he asked Eliza out on a date.

1. I have never seen Isla cry more bitterly than when she broke up with Carl.
2. Jay has a new coach now, and he is running faster than ever.
3. Mateo shouted more angrily than ever when he saw Zoe with someone else.
4. Fleur can talk to Ben more openly than to anyone else. He understands her.
5. Victoria's boyfriend is really good at school, so she is working much harder now.
6. Uncle Bert should really drive more slowly. It's dangerous to drive that fast.

S. 64 – 65 Words and Grammar: A terrible date

1. Sorry, I nearly forgot our date!
2. Don't worry; you're going to like it.
3. Do you like action films?
4. We should watch the new Bruce Willis film together.
5. Would you like to try my food?
6. You shouldn't have any dessert.

1. Zevi asks if I like sushi.
2. He says that we are going to have some anyway.
3. Zevi asks whether I always wear sports clothes when I'm on a date.
4. Zevi says when he first met me, he didn't like me at all.
5. He says if I don't want my sushi, he'll eat it.
6. Zevi thinks that this date was a very good idea.

1. Jessalyn says that she wanted to say no at first.
2. She asks if I am paying for this dinner.
3. She says that she is the girl, so she is going to pick the film.
4. Jessalyn thinks that I have gained weight since she last saw me.
5. She wants to know if I still work at "that stupid comic book store".
6. Jessalyn thinks that the food here is terrible. She wants to know why I didn't choose a nice restaurant.

S. 66 – 67 Words and Grammar: What do they ask?

1. Juliet asks herself why Romeo has to be a Montague.
2. Capulet asks Juliet why she doesn't want to marry Count Paris.
3. Romeo asks Juliet whether she will marry him.
4. Friar Laurence asks Juliet how he can help her.
5. Romeo wonders if there is a way to stop the fighting.
6. Montague asks Capulet how they can become friends.

1. Juliet asks herself when Romeo will be back.
2. Capulet asks Juliet what she is going to wear to the party tonight.
3. Romeo asks Juliet if she loves him.
4. Friar Laurence asks Juliet whether she is ready to take the drug.
5. Romeo wonders why their families have to be enemies.
6. Capulet asks Montague if he knew about Romeo and Juliet.

1. Juliet asks herself if her father will make her marry Count Paris.
2. Capulet asks Juliet who she was just talking to.
3. Romeo asks Juliet if she can forget his name.
4. Friar Laurence asks Juliet if she wants to leave Verona with Romeo.
5. Romeo wonders if Juliet will still love him.
6. Capulet asks Montague how they can ever forgive themselves.

S. 68 Speaking: Let's talk about Romeo and Juliet

Lösungsvorschlag:

Romeo and Juliet is a very famous love story by William Shakespeare. It's about two young lovers whose families are enemies. They meet when Romeo goes to a party at Juliet's parents' house. They fall in love and marry secretly the next day. But then Romeo kills Juliet's cousin in a fight and he has to leave Verona. Juliet's parents, who don't know that she is married, want her to marry someone else. She takes a drug to make her family think that she is dead. When Romeo comes back and finds her, he thinks that she really is dead, and he kills himself. Juliet wakes up to find her dead lover next to her, and she kills herself too. The two families then finally stop fighting.

Lösungsvorschlag:

The film *Titanic* is about two young people who meet on a ship on the journey to the USA. Jack is very poor, but Rose is from a rich family. She is very unhappy because she has to marry a man she doesn't love. Jack saves her when she tries to kill herself, and they fall in love, but her family are against their relationship. Rose decides to leave her family to be with Jack, but then there is an accident and the ship starts to sink. The story ends tragically because Jack dies in the cold water of the sea. Rose is rescued, but doesn't go back to her family and instead she starts a new life under a different name.

Lösungsvorschlag:
Romeo and Juliet is a famous play by William Shakespeare. It's about two young lovers whose families are enemies. They meet when Romeo goes to a party at Juliet's parents' house. They fall in love and marry secretly the next day. But then Romeo kills Juliet's cousin in a fight and has to leave Verona. Juliet's parents, who don't know that she is married, want her to marry someone else. She takes a drug to make her family think that she is dead. When Romeo comes back and finds her, he thinks that she really is dead, and he kills himself. Juliet wakes up to find her dead lover next to her, and she kills herself too. The two families then finally stop fighting.
The story is very dramatic and I liked it, even though the ending is very sad. I think it's a good story and it shows that terrible things can happen when people only see each other as enemies.

THEME 4: The world of work

S. 69 – 70 Listening: Stacey's work experience

a) Stacey is talking about her future job, her tasks during her work experience and her work experience at a hair salon.

b) 1. C 2. B 3. A 4. A 5. A 6. B

c) 1. right
2. right
3. wrong
4. right
5. wrong
6. right
7. wrong

d) 3. During her first week, Stacey had to make coffee or tea for customers, give them magazines and clean the floors.
5. Before you cut anyone's hair, you have to watch an experienced hairdresser many times.
7. Stacey would like to have her own hair salon one day.

e) 1. 18 people work at Fair Hair – 13 women and five men.
2. You have to make sure that the water isn't too hot or too cold.
3. Some customers were a little mean because Stacey was "just" doing her work experience.
4. She started work at 9 am and finished at 3 pm.

S. 71 – 73 Reading: Success can start in a garage

a) A A very big idea
B A changing world
C From the garage to Silicon Valley
D The centre of the Internet

b) 1. wrong
2. right
3. right
4. right
5. right
6. wrong
7. wrong
8. right

c) 1. In the 1940s, Stanford suddenly had too many students and needed money.
6. The area around San José has been called Silicon Valley since the early 1970s.
7. Silicon Valley is important today because it is the centre of high-tech, software and Internet companies.

d) 1. After the Second World War, many young men came home to the USA and wanted to study. The universities suddenly needed a lot of money to make that happen.
2. Stanford Industrial Park is only for high-tech companies.
3. In the 1980s, many small computer businesses became large companies and moved to Silicon Valley.
4. In the 1990s, the Internet became available to many people, so many new companies were founded in Silicon Valley.
5. Silicon Valley is known for its very good weather. There are 300 days of sunshine every year. Living there might be difficult for some people because Silicon Valley is also very expensive.

S. 74 Writing: My dream job

Lösungsvorschlag:
I would like to work as a gardener. I enjoy spending time outdoors, so I think the job would be perfect for me. As a gardener, you meet many different people and help them design their perfect garden. A gardener needs to know a lot about plants and help customers choose the right ones for their garden. You need good listening and communication skills and you should be able to work in a team. I think I would really enjoy all that.

S. 75 Writing: Hard skills and soft skills

Lösungsvorschlag:

I think that I am the right person for the job because I really like baking bread and cakes. Of course, if I get the job, I'll spend most of my time talking to customers and selling bread, but I think I would really learn a lot. I've got very good customer service and communication skills and I like working in a team. I have already done a work placement at a baker's and my boss was very happy with me. I also like getting up early, so the working hours won't be a problem for me. I'm always on time, and I would like to learn everything about the products so I can answer the customers' questions.

S. 76 Writing: The job interview

Lösungsvorschlag:

Mrs Muir: Welcome, Jessica. Thank you for coming here today.
You: Thank you for inviting me.
Mrs Muir: Do you have any work experience?
You: I did my work experience at a supermarket and I really enjoyed that.
Mrs Muir: What did you like about it?
You: I enjoyed helping the customers and answering their questions.
Mrs Muir: What are your favourite subjects in school?
You: I like maths and English, but I also enjoy PE.
Mrs Muir: Do you have any questions you would like to ask me?
You: Yes, I do. Would I work here in the morning or in the afternoon?
Mrs Muir: We're looking for someone to help out between 8 am and 11 am. Would that work for you?
You: Yes, of course.
Mrs Muir: Well, I think I'll see you on Saturday then.
You: Thank you very much.

S. 77 – 79 Mediation: 112 days in outer space

Lösungsvorschlag:

1. Yes, she is back now. She was in space for 112 days.
2. No, of course she wasn't! There were five other astronauts from different countries on the ISS with her.
3. Dr Gebauer says that she has always wanted to see the planet Earth from outer space.
4. She says that ESA, the European Space Agency, was looking for astronauts online six years ago. She had to try although she knew that you need a lot of luck because many people apply.

Lösungsvorschlag:

5. She was very happy and she says it was a great feeling. When she applied, she didn't think they would choose her, so she was surprised when she did. She hadn't even told her family that she wanted to be an astronaut.
6. Well, she says that astronauts can have different professions. There are pilots, engineers, scientists and doctors.
7. She says that you need to know about science. You shouldn't be stressed easily because you can't run away or hide on the ISS. You learn everything about being an astronaut during astronaut training.

Lösungsvorschlag:

8. Her job was to do different experiments. Scientists from all over Europe designed the experiments and she did them on the ISS. Sometimes she just had to push a button and see what happens, but other experiments were more complicated.
9. When she was in the American part of the ISS, she spoke English. She says that the astronauts learned from each other and tried to speak each other's languages a little. That was a lot of fun.

S. 80 Words and Grammar: Words, words, words

1. restaurant, café
2. doctor's office
3. plane
4. office
5. school
6. farm
7. garden
8. swimming pool, beach

There are many different jobs. A software developer has to develop new computer programmes. A plumber has to install heating systems. As a lifeguard, you must keep fit so you're able to rescue people. If you're not sure what kind of job is right for you, you should do one or more work placements to find out what you enjoy and what you are good at. You should try different jobs before you decide. Perhaps you would like to do training as a nurse or even study to become a doctor? Take your time and be patient, and you will find out what kind of job would be right for you.

verb	noun	verb	noun
train	training	develop	development
create	creation	produce	product/ production
release	release	offer	offer
result	result	demonstrate	demonstration

S. 81 Words and Grammar: Phrases

1. take a seat
2. give an example
3. sit down
4. apply for a job
5. fall asleep
6. improve your soft skills

S. 81 Words and Grammar: Skills

a)

hard skills	soft skills
typing	politeness
speaking different languages	ability to work in a team
computer programming	organizational skills
cooking	reliability

b) *Lösungsvorschlag:*

repairing cars	listening skills
school qualifications	being on time

c) *Lösungsvorschlag:*
One of my skills is politeness. For example, I always say hello and goodbye to people and I'm nice to them. Another of my skills is speaking different languages. I speak German and English, of course, and my mother is from Spain, so I also speak Spanish.
I also have cooking skills because we learn how to cook at school. I can make pancakes and soup, for example.
Finally, I've got good typing skills because we learned to type at school. I make very few mistakes and I'm quite fast.

S. 82 – 83 Words and Grammar: Career advice

1. If you are good at maths, you won't have any problems finding a job.
2. If you want to train as a web designer, you will have to apply for a job soon.
3. If you study medicine, you will take a lot of exams.
4. If you study abroad, you will improve your language skills.
5. If you want to work on your soft skills, you will find courses online.
6. If you are late for a job interview, you won't make a good impression.

1. If you become a scientist, you will do many interesting experiments.
2. If you go to university, you will need a lot of books.
3. If you work as a doctor's assistant, you will help people who are ill.
4. If you don't decide what you want to do soon, you won't have a job next summer.
5. If you don't find the right job, you won't enjoy your work.
6. If you write to that company, I'm sure they will invite you for a job interview.

1. If you work abroad for a year, you will meet many interesting people.
2. If you decide to study, you will learn some hard skills.
3. If you train as a nurse, you will not have easy working hours.
4. If you don't try harder, you will not find a job.
5. If you don't find a work placement soon, I will help you.
6. If you need help applying for a job, I will check your letter for you.

S. 83 – 84 Words and Grammar: Jobs and duties

1. A doctor should be nice to his or her patients if they are scared.
2. A gardener must be able to tell you a lot about different plants.
3. A software developer has to spend a lot of time at the office.
4. A hairdresser doesn't have to work late at night.
5. A police officer mustn't let anyone get away with stolen things.
6. A lifeguard is allowed to tell people to leave the swimming pool.

1. A nurse shouldn't be afraid of seeing some bad injuries.
2. My grandfather was a firefighter. He often had to deal with dangerous situations.
3. My sister wants to work in a bank later. She won't be allowed to talk about her customers' money to other people.
4. A doctor must be able to remember a lot of facts about the human body.
5. When my grandmother was a child, teachers were allowed to hit the pupils.
6. Our neighbour is a flight attendant. He can tell you lots of stories about different countries.

1. A teacher can/is allowed to/has to give the pupils homework.
2. In 1850, women were not allowed to become doctors.
3. A musician mustn't/shouldn't forget the words of a song during a concert.
4. An artist has to have a lot of ideas.

5. A flight attendant isn't allowed to/mustn't fly a plane.
6. A secretary doesn't have to be able to swim.

S. 85 – 86 Words and Grammar: If only ...

1. If Eliza tidied her room more often, she would spend less time looking for things.
2. If Becca believed in herself more, her soft skills would be much better.
3. If Mika used his computer for school, he would develop some useful skills.
4. If Liv concentrated more, she would get much better marks.
5. If Greg went to France, it would help him with his language skills.
6. If Miles trained a little harder, he would play tennis well enough to become a professional.

1. If Jack spent less time playing hockey, he would have more time for his homework.
2. If Hannah applied for a work placement at the hotel, I'm sure they would invite her for an interview.
3. If Joshua wasn't so nervous, his job interviews would go better.
4. If Katie didn't have such good marks, she wouldn't be able to train to become a software developer.
5. If Chloe left the house a little earlier, she wouldn't get into trouble for being late every day.
6. If Matthew developed his communication skills, he would find a job more easily.

Lösungsvorschlag:
1. If Ellie had an afternoon job, she would have more money.
2. If Callum did his homework every day, he would understand his lessons better.
3. If Lewis had more pocket money, he would buy a new bike.
4. If Connor improved his soft skills, he would find a work placement more easily.
5. If Grace found someone to help with her history presentation, she would feel less nervous about it.
6. If Charlotte took part in the maths competition at school, I'm sure she would win.

S. 86 – 87 Words and Grammar: Work experience

1. Miranda said that she was doing her work experience as a secretary.
2. Kalen and Keira said that they were happy to work together.
3. Ben said that his work experience was really boring.
4. Kimberly said that she was learning a lot at the doctor's office.
5. Abdul said that his boss was teaching him a lot about the job.
6. Jeff said that he would ask if he could work there in the summer.

1. Violet said that she was thinking about becoming a doctor's assistant.
2. Chang said that he had to be at work at 7.30 am.
3. Mila said that she didn't want to work as a hairdresser anymore.
4. Linus said that dealing with customers could be really hard sometimes.
5. Alexei said that he couldn't wait to go back to school.
6. Riya said that she hoped she could work there again during the summer.

a) 1. Nigel said that he would be sorry when his work experience was over.
2. Vasili said that he didn't understand why they had to do work experience.
3. Daria said that she was having a really good time.

b) 1. Victoria: "I really enjoy feeling useful."
2. Katherine: "Some of my tasks are a little boring."
3. Ryan: "I'm going to apply for a job as a gardener after school."

S. 88 Speaking: The right job

Lösungsvorschlag:

A: Hello, B. Can I ask for your advice?
B: Hello, A. Of course! How can I help you?
A: I'm trying to decide what kind of job might be right for me.
B: Well, what are you good at? I mean, what school subjects do you like, for example?
A: I like PE, but my favourite subject is maths.
B: As far as I know, you're also good at English, right? And you like working with people.
A: That's true. I think I've also got good computer skills.
B: That's good. You enjoy working on difficult tasks, right?
A: Yes, I do. I like solving problems. You know, I did work experience as a mechanic, but I didn't really like it too much. Have you already done work experience?

B: Yes, I have. I worked for an engineer. That was really interesting and I learned a lot. Have you ever thought about becoming an engineer?
A: That sounds interesting. I have always dreamed of working on big projects. I think I should do a different work experience. What do you think?
B: I think that is a good idea. I can give you my boss's number – perhaps you can do work experience there.

THEME 5: Away from home

S. 89 – 90 Listening: Mr Goldman

☆ ☾ ☼ a) A4 B5 C1 D2

☾ ☼ b) 1. C 2. B 3. A 4. C 5. B 6. B 7. B 8. A

☼ c) 1. They have invited Mr Goldman as part of their project on immigration.
2. Mr Goldman was born in 1932.
3. They left because they are Jewish and they had problems with the Nazis.
4. Mrs Rubenstein was Mr Goldman's mother's best friend.
5. The journey took about two weeks.
6. They only had a very small room and they had to share the toilet with many other people.
7. The first thing Mr Goldman saw was the Statue of Liberty.
8. Mr Goldman says that there are no words to describe how happy he was.

S. 91 – 93 Reading: A German immigrant in the USA

☆ ☾ ☼ a) A4 B5 C1 D7 E2 F3

☾ ☼ b) 1. A 2. C 3. B 4. A 5. B 6. B

☼ c) 1. As a child, he liked listening to music, reading poems, and painting.
2. He worked as a farmer for some years.
3. Roebling and his wife Johanna had nine children together. The first, Washington, was born in 1837.
4. The John A. Roebling Suspension Bridge was the longest suspension bridge in the world for some time.
5. Emily Warren Roebling helped her husband finish the Brooklyn Bridge. She learned about mathematics and engineering, even though women couldn't yet become engineers at the time.
6. After John A. Roebling's death, it took 14 years to finish the Brooklyn Bridge.
7. Building the Brooklyn Bridge cost about $15.5 million. In today's money, that would be nearly $400 million.

S. 94 Writing: My life as an exchange student

☆ *Lösungsvorschlag:*
Hello everybody,
After a year in New Jersey, I am now back home.
I lived with a very nice family: Bob and Jessica and their children, Eric and Vanessa. I went to high school every day, joined the basketball team and played in the school band.
At first, I missed my family and friends back home a little, but then I really enjoyed everything.
My American family took me on many trips.
I'm happy to be back with my own family now, but I really miss my American family and friends.

S. 95 Writing: A natural disaster

☾ *Lösungsvorschlag:*
Dear diary,
There has been a bad flood in our town. Our house has been badly damaged and we have to stay with my grandparents for some time. I can only take a few clothes, my schoolbooks and my smartphone. Many of our things have been destroyed. Luckily, we can take our dog and cat with us. They're OK, but very frightened. I'm frightened, too, but my parents say that I shouldn't worry. We will wait until all of the water has gone and then we will take a look at our house. I really hope we can go home soon.

S. 96 Writing: A new chance

☼ *Lösungsvorschlag:*
Dear Pablo,
I'm sorry I didn't tell you that we were leaving Mexico. We decided to cross the border into the USA because my parents can't find jobs at home. We walked through the desert and crossed the border at night. We had to run fast because the Border Patrol is never far away. I'm glad we made it here, but I'm worried, too. I hope that my parents will find good jobs soon. At the moment, we are staying with my aunt, but her apartment is very small. Perhaps I can go to school here. I really want to go to university later so I can get a good job and help my parents. Hopefully nobody will find us and send us back.
Yours,
Enrique

S. 97 – 98 Mediation: José's story

1. Er lebt in einer Stadt namens Laredo, in Texas. Das ist in der Nähe der mexikanischen Grenze.
2. Nein, er selbst ist in den USA geboren, deshalb ist er Amerikaner.
3. Josés Eltern sind beide Mexikaner.
4. Seine Eltern und Geschwister sind vor 25 Jahren in die USA gekommen.
5. Sie haben sich entschieden, zu gehen, weil es in Mexiko viele Probleme gab. Sie waren sehr arm, sein Vater hatte keine Arbeit und seine Mutter verdiente sehr wenig. Es war auch sehr gefährlich in Mexiko wegen der Drogen und der Kriminalität.

6. Sie haben beschlossen, durch die Wüste zu gehen. Sie wollten der Grenzstreife aus dem Weg gehen.
7. Sie hatten gehört, dass viele wegen der Hitze in der Wüste gestorben waren, deshalb sind sie nachts gegangen und haben viel Wasser mitgenommen.
8. José wurde 1997 geboren.
9. Er sagt, dass sie ganz normale Teenager waren. Sie hatten gute Noten, José hat Fußball gespielt und seine Schwester war Cheerleaderin.
10. Sein Vater arbeitet als Ingenieur und seine Mutter im Büro eines Restaurants.

11. José sagt, dass es für ihn einfach ist, weil er Amerikaner ist. Er will auf die Universität gehen.
12. Sie haben immer Angst, nach Mexiko zurückgeschickt zu werden, weil sie illegale Einwanderer sind.
13. Er wurde von der Polizei angehalten, weil er zu schnell gefahren ist. Zum Glück haben die Polizisten ihm nur gesagt, er solle langsamer fahren.
14. José meint, dass es besser wäre, wenn seine Eltern und Geschwister Green Cards hätten.
15. Er sagt, dass viele Amerikaner weniger Einwanderung in die USA wollen.

S. 99 Words and Grammar: Odd one out

1. destroy
2. once
3. immigration
4. pain
5. political
6. opinion

S. 99 Words and Grammar: Definitions

1. emigrate
2. gift
3. caption
4. escape
5. journey
6. hope

Lösungsvorschlag:

1. war: a big and very bad fight between two or more countries or groups of people
2. university: a place where you can study after finishing school
3. racist: a person who doesn't like some people because of the colour of their skin or where they are from
4. government: the group of people who run a country
5. sick: another word for 'ill'
6. rent: the money that you must pay every month if you don't own the house or flat you live in

S. 100 Words and Grammar: Word lists

a)

people or things	what you can do	how things/ people can be
government	destroy	extreme
racist	emigrate	impossible
war	reach	racist
university	announce	sick
education	feed	political

b) *Lösungsvorschlag:*

writer	return	stormy
gift	move	crowded

c) *Lösungvorschlag:*

1. Many people must leave their homes because there is a war in their country.
2. Every child has the right to an education.
3. In the 19th century, many Irish people emigrated and went to the USA.
4. My favourite band has announced that their new album is coming out soon.
5. It is impossible to turn water into gold.
6. The political situation in many countries is very difficult.
7. If you want to go to university, you should work hard at school.
8. Extreme storms can destroy whole cities.

S. 101 – 102 Words and Grammar: A famous immigrant

1. When Arnold Schwarzenegger <u>had finished</u> school in Austria, he joined the army.
2. After he <u>had left</u> the army, he concentrated on sport.
3. Before Schwarzenegger went to the USA, he <u>had won</u> several bodybuilding competitions in Austria.

4. After he had moved to the USA, he began to work on his career there.
5. When he had learned enough English, he took classes at university.
6. When Schwarzenegger had lived in the USA for 15 years, he became an American.

☾ 1. Arnold Schwarzenegger had played football for many years before he became a bodybuilder.
2. When he had done bodybuilding for a while, he stopped playing football.
3. When Schwarzenegger had won the important 'Mr Universe' competition twice, his international career started.
4. After he had ended his bodybuilding career, he decided to become an actor.
5. After he had played some small roles on television, he became a big Hollywood film star.
6. Schwarzenegger had been in a relationship with Maria Shriver for nearly nine years when they married in 1986.

☼ 1. After people had seen some of Arnold Schwarzenegger's films, they accepted him as an actor.
2. After Schwarzenegger had worked as an actor for many years, he went into politics.
3. When he had won the election to become Governor of California in 2006, he tried to do good things for nature.
4. Before he ended his career in politics, he had announced that he wanted to make films again.
5. Before he acted in a big film project again, he had tested if his fans still liked him.
6. After Schwarzenegger and Maria Shriver had been married for 25 years, they broke up.

S. 103 – 104 Words and Grammar: Before and after

☆ 1. Before the Europeans came, only Native Americans had lived in North America.
2. After many people had died in the potato famine, lots of Irish people emigrated to the USA.
3. When the new immigration station at Ellis Island had opened, all the new immigrants had to pass through it.
4. Before they arrived at Ellis Island, people had spent weeks on ships.
5. When immigration officers and doctors had checked them, the immigrants were allowed to go to New York.
6. After the immigrants had found somewhere to live, they built a new life for themselves in the USA.

☾ 1. After Jessica had finished school, she worked in England for a year.
2. Before she decided to go abroad, she had talked to her family and friends about it.
3. When she had thought about everything for a while, she applied for a student job.
4. After she had taken a language test, she went to England for a job interview.
5. When she had done some training, she started her new job.
6. After she had spent a year in England, she spoke English very well.

☼ 1. The government had warned the people before the hurricane hit the town.
2. The people had bought lots of food and water before the storm arrived.
3. After the storm had destroyed their homes, the people built new houses.
4. The people in Syria had lived normal lives before the war began.
5. After their homes had been destroyed in the war, many people went to Europe.
6. When they had found new homes in Europe, they tried to start a new life.

S. 105 Speaking: A new life

☆ ☾ *Lösungsvorschlag:*

I can see a lot of people who have just arrived at a train station. There are some young men and a family with small children. The people are wearing jeans and jackets, and they are carrying bags. Somebody is giving one of the children a teddy bear. Perhaps the people are refugees who have just arrived in Germany. I think they could be from Syria, for example. They look happy, but also a little tired.

☼ *Lösungsvorschlag:*

I can see a lot of people who have just arrived at a train station. There are some young men and a family with small children. The people are wearing jeans and jackets, and they are carrying bags. Somebody is giving one of the children a teddy bear. Perhaps the people are refugees who have just arrived in Germany. I think they could be from Syria, for example. They look happy, but also a little tired. If I were in their situation, I would also feel a little nervous about what is going to happen next. I'm sure they are going to miss their home and perhaps they will want to go back some day, but for now, they are probably happy to be safe.

Texte zu den Hörverstehensaufgaben auf der CD

Track	Theme	Titel	Spielzeit
1	Theme 1: Welcome to the USA	American food	3:03
2	Theme 2: Challenges	My biggest challenge	2:57
3	Theme 3: Love and friendship	*West Side Story*	3:32
4	Theme 4: The world of work	Stacey's work experience	3:09
5	Theme 5: Away from home	Mr Goldman	3:26
6	Theme 5: Away from home	José's story	3:03

THEME 1: Welcome to the USA

zu S. 6 – 7: American food

Rachel: Hi! I'm working on a school project on typical American food. Do you have two minutes?

Karen: Yeah, no problem. I'm Karen. What do you want to know?

Rachel: What food do you usually eat?

Karen: Oh, wow … let me think. Yesterday I had cornflakes for breakfast. For lunch I had a fresh salad with tomatoes and cheese. And last night I made rice with vegetables and a tomato sauce.

Rachel: What would you say is typical American food?

Karen: Maybe a burger with fries, but that isn't very healthy. I prefer good food. I cook a fresh meal every night because I think it's important to take the time, sit down and eat. I buy a lot of organic food at the local farmers' market. The fruit and vegetables there are fresh and very tasty.

Rachel: Thank you, Karen! … Excuse me, sir, can I ask you a few questions for a school project?

Jacques: If you think I can help you … I'm a tourist from Paris. My name is Jacques.

Rachel: Hello, Jacques! What food do you eat here in New York?

Jacques: Um … I had a bagel for breakfast yesterday, and a turkey sandwich for lunch. Later, I went for dinner with some friends and we had amazing Chinese food at a small restaurant.

Rachel: What do you know about typical American food?

Jacques Well, for me American food means burgers, hot dogs and steaks. New York is special because there's food from so many different countries.

Rachel: Thank you! … Excuse me, do you have two minutes?

Dennis: Sure thing! I'm Dennis.

Rachel: What did you eat yesterday?

Dennis: My mom always makes pancakes for breakfast. She says it's the most important meal of the day. I bought a cheese sandwich with some fries for lunch. And for dinner, my mom made pasta with cheese.

Rachel: What do you think is typical American food?

Dennis: My mom sometimes makes traditional dishes like meat loaf, or turkey for Thanksgiving. Me, I love fast food! There are so many fast food restaurants here. And you don't have to spend time cooking food.

Rachel: Aren't you worried about your health?

Dennis: Not really. I do a lot of sports. I guess it's expensive, but my mom gives me lunch money.

THEME 2: Challenges

zu S. 24 – 25: My biggest challenge

Tom: Hi! I'm Tom. This picture shows me at the local farmers' market. My parents and I have a big garden where we grow fruit and vegetables. We sell our products at the market and people love it because our stuff is organic. My dad lost his job a few months ago, so this way we can make a little money until he finds a new job. I'm really proud of my dad because he's trying so hard to find a job, but it's still a big challenge for the whole family.

Jenny: Um, my name's Jenny. Compared to your situation, mine is no big challenge, but my parents think that I can still be proud of what I do. This picture shows me at the supermarket. My grandmother has an apartment around the corner. She's getting older and it's difficult for her to carry heavy bags, so I go shopping for her twice a week. I take my bike so that I can buy more stuff. My grandmother says that it makes her feel happy because this way, she can still live in her own apartment, and I'm glad that I can help.

Pamela: I'm Pamela and my picture shows me on top of a mountain. I'm afraid of heights – I can't even stand on a chair to hang a picture or look down from a tall building. It's hard to deal with this alone, so I found a group of people who have the same problem. We challenged each other by climbing this mountain. It was really hard and I had to put all my energy into this project, but I made it up there! I was so proud of myself and all the others!

James: I'm James and my picture shows me throwing a pack of cigarettes away. I stopped smoking two months ago and I'm so glad I did! I started smoking when I was really young because I thought it was cool. I wanted to be part of a group and when I smoked, people accepted me and thought I was older. That made me feel good. It was really hard to quit. My family helped me, but I had to fight – I wanted a cigarette so badly! I finally made it, and now I'm really happy. I never want to smoke another cigarette ever again!

THEME 3: Love and friendship

zu S. 46 – 47: *West Side Story*

Teresa:

Well, um, our task was to prepare a presentation on famous love stories in theatre and film, and I chose the film *West Side Story*. Actually, it's not really a film. It was a musical first and it was first performed on Broadway in 1957. The film was made four years later, in 1961.

West Side Story is actually the first modern musical. There was music and dancing in the theatre before, but never like this. It's very difficult for actors because they have to dance, sing and act at the same time.

OK, um … A team of musicians and writers started to work on the musical in 1949 and called it *East Side Story*. The idea was to make a modern version of *Romeo and Juliet*, but instead of two families, there are two gangs that fight. Actually, um, there were real gang fights between different groups in American cities at the time, so you can see that part is quite realistic. The musical won two Tony Awards in 1958. The Tony Awards are like the Oscars, but for theatre.

As I said, the musical was soon made into a film. It made almost 44 million dollars, but it only cost 6 million dollars to make. The film also won ten Oscars, for example for the Best Film and the Best Music.

There are 18 songs in *West Side Story*. Leonard Bernstein wrote the music and Stephen Sondheim wrote the lyrics. They were both unhappy with the film version because it changed some of the music. Both the film and the musical are still very popular today. The Community Drama Club is preparing a run of ten performances at the moment. The first performance will actually be in … wait … right, the week before Christmas, so if you're interested, perhaps you'll go. Tickets cost £10 and children under 8 pay nothing. The Community Centre is going to use the money to build a new playground, so hopefully many people will come to see the musical. After all, I think it's a fantastic story!

OK, thank you for listening. I hope I didn't forget anything important.

THEME 4: The world of work

zu S. 69 – 70: Stacey's work experience

Teenage reporter: Hello and good morning everyone! We're going to talk to a ninth-year student who has just come back from her two-week work experience. Here with me in the studio is Stacey Thomas. Stacey, could you please tell our listeners where you did your work experience?

Stacey: I did my work experience at Fair Hair. It's a big hairdressing salon in the city centre.

Reporter: How many people work at Fair Hair?

Stacey: There are 18 hairdressers, 13 women and five men. It's a young team and they're all very friendly.

Reporter: What did you do there?

Stacey: At first, I did jobs like making coffee or tea for customers or bringing them magazines. I had to clean the floors as well. At the end of my first week I was allowed to wash hair, too. You have to be very careful that the water isn't too hot or too cold.

Reporter: I see. So, what did you do in your second week?

Stacey: In the second week, I helped to colour hair. It's a difficult job because it takes a long time and you have to be very careful that the colour doesn't get on people's skin or clothes.

Reporter: Sounds like you learned a lot about the job in the two weeks.

Stacey: Yes, that's for sure. And I really liked it!

Reporter: How do hairdressers actually learn to cut hair?

Stacey: You have to watch an experienced hairdresser many times. Later, the salon will offer free haircuts to people who let you practise on their hair.

Reporter: Sounds interesting. Was there anything you didn't like?

Stacey: Well, some of the customers were a little arrogant when they learned that I was "just" doing my work experience there. Also, my feet sometimes hurt because you have to stand all day.

Reporter: What were your working hours?

Stacey: I started work at nine and finished at three. I had one long break for lunch and two short breaks of 15 minutes each.

Reporter: Do you think you would like to become a hairdresser some day?

Stacey: Yes, I think I would! And I'd like to have my own hair salon one day.

Reporter: Thanks for talking to us, Stacey.

Stacey: Thank you.

Reporter: Next up we're going to talk about the school dance next week. The theme is going to be …

THEME 5: Away from home

zu S. 89 – 90 Mr Goldman

Teacher: Good morning everybody! As part of our project on immigration we have invited Mr Goldman here today. Welcome, Mr Goldman!

Mr Goldman: Thank you for inviting me.

Teacher: We've been talking about immigration for a few weeks now. Rizwan, can you tell us what we've learned so far?

Rizwan: Immigrants have come to the USA from all over the world and for many different reasons. We talked about the many immigrants from Great Britain and Ireland. I saw a film about Ireland in the 19th century. People died of hunger and there were no jobs. Those who could left for America.

Teacher: Yes, that's right. Let's talk to Mr Goldman now. Mr Goldman, where are you from originally?

Mr Goldman: I'm from Germany. We lived in Berlin and my dad owned a small shop there.

Teacher: Mr Goldman, when and why did you and your family come to the USA?

Mr Goldman: That was a long time ago. I was born in 1932, so I'm quite old now. My parents, my sister and I left Germany in 1938, so I can't remember much of Germany. I was only six years old. But my father told me that we fled from Germany because of the Nazis. We had lots of problems because we're Jewish.

Rizwan: Why did you choose America?

Mr Goldman: Our neighbors, the Rubensteins, had family in New York. Mrs Rubenstein was my mother's best friend. She told my parents all about America and how great it was. Mr and Mrs Rubenstein had already left Germany the year before.

Teacher: How did you get here?

Mr Goldman: We came by ship from Hamburg to New York. The journey took about two weeks, and it wasn't very nice. We only had a very small room and we had to share the toilet with many other people. It was stormy and I felt sick all the time. I thought the journey would never end.

Teacher: What was the first thing you saw when you arrived in New York?

Mr Goldman: We arrived in New York early in the morning, the sun had just come up and there it was in the morning light: the Statue of Liberty. She was so beautiful! I remember it as if it were today. Then we all knew: We had made it to America. There are no words that can describe that feeling of happiness.

zu S. 97 – 98: José's story

Hi there! My name is José Menendez and I'm from Laredo, Texas. That's a city close to the Mexican border. I'm a Mexican-American. My parents are Mexicans, but I was born in the United States, so I'm an American.
My parents came here 25 years ago with my brother and sister. My family left Mexico because there were lots of problems there. They were very poor, my father didn't have a job and my mother earned very little money. Life was also very dangerous in Mexico because of drugs and crime. My parents planned to cross the border in the desert to avoid the U.S. Border Patrol. Lots of people had died trying to get into the USA because of the heat in the desert, so my family decided to walk at night and to take lots of water with them. They were lucky and made it across the border. Five years later, in 1997, I was born here in Laredo. My brother, sister and I have always lived the lives of typical American teenagers. We had good grades in school, I played soccer on the school team and my sister was a cheerleader. My father works as an engineer and my mom works in the office at a restaurant. I'll go to university one day and life is very easy for me because I'm an American. But my parents and my brother and sister are here illegally. They always live in fear of being sent back to Mexico. A few months ago, my father was stopped by the police because he was driving a little too fast. Luckily they just told him to drive more slowly. It's really hard for me when I see that they're always scared of being caught by the police. Everyday life is harder for them, too. Without the right papers, it's difficult to find work. My brother and sister both went to university, but they can't get a job. I really hope they'll all get Green Cards one day so they'll have easier lives – just like me. Then they can live and work in the USA as long as they want. But that seems almost impossible now because many Americans want less immigration to the USA.